JN078629

関西詩人協会　日本語・英語アンソロジー

言葉の花火　2021

FIREWORK POEMS VIII

関西詩人協会　日本語・英語アンソロジー

言葉の花火　2021

FIREWORK POEMS VIII

An Anthology of Japanese and English Bilingual Poems
from Kansai Poets' Association

Foreword

I pen this with the whole world affected by the COVID-19 pandemic. Here in Japan, we are in and out of national states of emergency and with no clear way ahead in sight.

Under these present circumstances, Kansai Poets' Association is publishing the eighth volume of its triennial bilingual anthology of *Firework Poems*, which makes it twenty-four years since the first volume was produced. We may ask ourselves what is to be done when people are being urged to stay home and personal contact and socialization greatly frustrated. And yet, as an assembly of poets, we are fortunate to have the freedom to pursue the business of our writing. Indeed, one might go as far as to say that it is the poet's duty to reach out to a world suffering from this common pandemic curse.

I often find myself reflecting on the nature of language, and coming to the conclusion that it is a bridge that links individuals who share a common humanity, thus breaching the distances that separate us by reaching out to other shores. It is sincerely hoped that the creative passion of the present anthology will become such a bridge and reach the breasts of its unknown readers — like a rainbow of hope.

Finally, I wish to express my gratitude and respect to Yakushigawa Koichi, Kitaoka Takeshi, Saitoh Akinori, Mizusaki Noriko and Yamamoto Yumiko, the five members of our Association who undertook the translation; to Norman Angus who has aided the project since the publication of the first volume; the editors of the present anthology, Tsukasa Yui and Nako Kiyoe; and to all the poets without whose contributions this book would not be possible. You have, one and all, my personal and deepest thanks.

Chief Director of Kansai Poets' Association
SAKO Mayumi

はじめに

　世界中が新型コロナウイルスのパンデミックに覆われているなか、これを書いています。日本では緊急事態宣言が出たり解除されたりの繰り返しで、なかなか先の見えない現状です。

　そんな今、関西詩人協会の日・英語翻訳詩集『言葉の花火』は第8集を出版する運びとなりました。三年に一度の出版ですので、第一集からはや24年を経過したことになります。ステイホームを強いられ、人と人とが集うことがままならない今、できることは何か。幸いわたしたちは詩人の団体ですので、書くことだけは自由です。そして、コロナ禍の今、同じような苦しみを味わっている世界に向けて発信することは、詩人の使命であるかもしれません。

　「ことば」とは何かとよく思います。ことばは人と人とを結ぶ橋、同じ人間同士として、思いを共有するために、離れた別々の岸を結ぶようにことばはあるのでしょう。ここに書かれた創作者の熱意が橋となって誰かの胸に届きますように。そして、願わくは、希望の虹の架け橋となりますように、願ってやみません。

　最後になりましたが、この本の出版にあたって、翻訳に携わってくださった5名の会員の方々、薬師川虹一・北岡武司・斉藤明典・水崎野里子・山本由美子の各氏に、第一集から並々ならぬご尽力をいただいているノーマン・アンガス先生、そして編集にあたってくださった司由衣、名古きよえの各氏、参加してくださった詩人のみなさまに心から感謝と敬意を表したいと思います。誠にありがとうございました。

関西詩人協会代表
左子真由美

CONTENTS

言葉の花火　2021 FIREWORK POEMS Ⅷ

ARIMA Takashi

The Lord of Creation

Normally we strut proudly about on our two legs,
But none of us can tell when our time will be up.
This time it's the coronavirus,
Going this way and going that,
Who knows who might suddenly drop down?

Do it! — Wear a face mask!
No unventilated rooms, no gatherings, and keep your distance!
Self-important experts bossing us around.
Even the politicians who discuss the world and its states,
Wait to see how the situation will unfold,
Asking with folded arms what is to be done.

The elderly and the young
Get more and more irritated —
Bring back normality soon!
No, not yet. It's too early.
The bottom line, as long as you wear a mask,
Is that things will somehow settle down.

And yet, when I hear about the vital vaccine,
The response is never clear,
And no one knows when we will get it.
Does it mean that, against this unknown virus,
We should eat a pickled plum in the morning,
And suck a throat drop in the evening?
Now that's what I call the lord of creation.

万物の霊長

ふだんは威張って二本足で歩いているが
その人間もいつ死ぬかわからん
こんどは新型コロナの一件で
右往左往して
いつなんどき　コロリといくかもしれん

やれ　マスクをしろとか
密閉　密集　密接　はあかんとか
専門家にえらそうなこと言われて
天下国家を論じる政治家さえも
まわりの様子をうかがって
どうしたもんか　と腕組みしとる

年寄りも　若いものも
イライラがつのって
早く通常にもどせ
いや　早過ぎる
とにかく　マスクさえしておれば
なんとか落ちついてくるにちがいない

しかし肝心のワクチンの話を聞くと
答えはいつもあいまいで
いつまでにできるのかはっきりしない
これでは未知のウイルスには
朝がたは梅干しを食べて
夕がたにはのど飴をねぶっておれ　ということか
万物の霊長らしく

Kyoko 2021 — Come Spring! Come Buddha!

The melancholic Kyoko, now passed away, was my wife, my lady.
We met at a study group of the same generation;
The depression worsened, and she took her life in 2016,
At the age of 37.
Upwards and upwards,
She was born again.
But on Valentine's Day, 2014, I stayed at her house —
The court had decreed we divorce for mutual health reasons,
But I was happy.
I came to her as if drawn, and she to her separated husband as her
    only life line.
Kissing Kyoko, as only she could be, on the *futon* in front of the
    family altar,
Kisses I still remember,
As my tongue caressed her lower neck,
And Kyoko's faint voice whispering, "That feels so good, Shou-chan."
Our legs crossed as I pushed inwards;
In the flow, Kyoko licked my toes,
And I licked hers —
The two of us like electric wires.
Was I giving her pleasure — me who has always been rejected?
An advertisement in one of the Buddhist weeklies say:
Suicide is a renunciation of life's assignment,
So those who do it return as themselves to try again.
Ah, Kyoko, snuggling like a child, your Shou-chan will die for you
    if something happens.
Then we can meet again in the same parallel hours of our past —
Me the same good-looking guy, and Kyoko the same unchanged girl —
Down and down, from failure to failure.

Ah, the distant spring and our distant Buddha!
Closing my eyes, I can hear your sweet voice —
Come spring! Come Buddha!

京子二〇二一 ～ 春よ来い、仏よ来い ～

同年代の〇〇学会をやっていた元妻、うつ病の京子、私の女でした
うつ病の悪化
二〇一六年、自殺しました
享年三七
上へ上へ
産まれ変わりました
二〇一四年のバレンタインの夜、京子の家でお泊まり
互いの病気のため、裁判所からの通知で政治的に離婚措置になった元
　妻なのに
僕は幸せだった
吸い付くように元妻の元へ、元夫しかいないと京子も
京子特有の御本尊さまの前の布団でちゅうちゅう
印象に憶えているちゅうちゅうは
京子の首の下を「翔ちゃん」が舐めていると
弱い声で「気持ちいい」と言った
「翔ちゃん」が挿入しながら、脚を交差した
京子は自然と彼の脚の指を舐めた
彼も京子の脚の指を自然と舐めた
電気配線の二人
あちこちで、嫌われ者の僕の存在が気持ちよかったのか
自殺したら仏教（真言宗系新宗教）の週刊文春の広告が言う
『人生の宿題の放棄』だから
もう一度、同じ自分でやり直すと描いてあった
甘えん坊の京子よ、翔ちゃんも君のためにいつかなんかあったら自殺
　してあげよう
同じパラレルワールドの過去の時間の中で再び逢おう
同じ自分のイケメンの顔、同じ京子の顔
下へ下へ、失敗へ失敗へ

遠き春よ、遠き仏よ、まぶた閉じればそこに
懐かしい君の声がする
春よ来い、仏よ来い
愛をくれしき君の懐かしき声がする

Crisis

This new virus that has gnawed the world's sun
Has made not just our life but also our hearts jagged

Our faces covered with masks
Our expressions unreadable
Our speech unconsciously reduced
And like women in some cultures
Our real faces shown only to the intimate

We refrain from gathering
And keep our distance from the you in front of me
Even the handshake
Forbidden

Before we know it the season has changed
The song of insects has faded away
The cosmos have ceased to bloom
And on the forecast chart
Snowmen start to appear

The sky we look up at is high
And cold air brushes my cheek

In gratitude to our healthcare workers and researchers
I release a paper plane of hope into the current of the air
Soon, beyond that cloud,
You should be able to see it

禍

遠藤カズエ

世界の〈太陽〉を齧った新型ウィルスは
人々の生活様式や心までギザギザにした

顔はマスクで覆い
表情は読みとれない
いつの間にか言葉も少なく
某国の女性のように
親しい人にしか素顔を見せなくなった

集うことを自粛し
目の前のあなたと距離を置き
してはいけない
Handshake

気がつけば季節は巡り
虫の聲が遠のき
コスモスも咲き終え
天気予報図に
雪だるまの画を目にするようになった

見上げる空は高い
冷気がピシリと頬を打つ

私は医療従事者や研究者に感謝を込めて
気流に乗れよと紙飛行機を飛ばす
あの雲の向こうに
もうすぐ光が見えるはず

A Grain of Sand

(1)

A single grain of sand
Proves the existence of the universe.

A single grain of sand
Equals the expansion of a billion years.

A single grain of sand
Amounts to all the abundance of water.

And that you are
Means that a future exists.

(2)

That you are a tree standing in a wind of sorrow means
Your innumerable selves are a tree standing in a wind of sorrow.

That you, under the darkness which shrouds you,
Would spread your frail wings, and fly into the azure sky of the heart is
The myriads of you, under the darkness which shrouds you,
Spreading their frail wings and flying into the azure sky of the heart.

That towards tomorrow, embraced in distress and pain,
You will walk on at the point between life and death is
Your irreplaceable and innumerable selves ticking away
Second by second in the time of the universe.

And all this means that, as if falling from eternity to become a grain
    of sand,
And delving to the source of life, you are praying to transcend
    yourself.

一粒の砂

藤谷恵一郎

（一）
一粒の砂があるということは
宇宙があるということ

一粒の砂があるということは
億年の時の広がりがあるということ

一粒の砂があるということは
豊かな水があるということ

君がいるということは
未来があるということ

（二）
あなたが悲しみの風に立つ一本の樹木であるということは
無数のあなたが悲しみの風に立つ一本の樹木であるということ

あなたがあなたを覆う闇の下で　心の青空に
痩せこけた羽交いの翼を広げ　翔けようとすることは
無数のあなたがあなたを覆う闇の下で　心の青空に
痩せこけた羽交いの翼を広げ　翔けようとすること

あなたが苦悩と苦痛に抱かれ
明日へ命の時を歩もうとしていることは
かけがえのない無数のあなたが
宇宙の時の一秒一秒を刻んでいるということ

そして　永遠から落ちるように一粒の砂となり　命の源を潜り
あなた自体へと超出することを祈っているということ

FUKUDA Kei

The Lion of The West House

My father, born in 1895, inherited the main house and a separate one
    from his family
The second house was five minutes on foot to the west
And we called this residence, where no one lived, the West House.

For a long time, long before I was born, a white stone lion with a powerfully
    carved mane sat in the front garden with its grand camphor tree.
He dominated the large garden with his deep eyes, great mouth, sturdy legs,
    and shining silver torso, and round him was a circle of pebbles, and white
    and red camellias, nandina bushes, a maple, and flowering leopard plants
    all bending round.
In the fall, the coloured leaves and, in the winter, the falling snow piled upon
    his head
Yet he kept his usual silence and never flinched.
When I was little, I put red nandina berries into his eyes
And often got on top of him to play.
Each day one of the family would visit
So he was monarch of the West House, watching over it through wind and snow.
From time to time, friends who came to play would sketch him from the sun porch
And he was often photographed just sitting there in the garden
His very presence calming our minds.

The day after I got married, my father collapsed at the front door and was
    confined to bed
Eight years of this passed
And fearing the lion might devour the houses' owner, he was removed.
Not long after, father passed away and the Edo period
House of the West demolished, and two new houses built on the site for my brothers.

They say he now rests in the garden of a large mansion
At Nukata Station on the Kintetsu Nara Line.
How I wish someone would lift me up once more onto the king's torso
Cold, shining, and silver!

西の家のライオン

福田ケイ

　　　明治28年生まれの父は　先祖から本宅と別宅を受け継ぎ
　　　本宅から　西に歩いて5分の所に別宅があった
　　　誰も住んでいない　この屋敷を家族は　西の家と呼んでいた

私が生まれるずっと昔から　大木のくすの木のある西の家の
前栽には白い石のライオンが座っていた　鋭く彫られた長いたて髪
深い眼　大きな口　どっしりした足　胴体は銀色に輝き　広い庭を
支配していた　白と赤の椿の木や　南天の木　紅葉　つわぶきの
花がライオンによりそい　玉石が彼のまわりを囲んでいた
秋には枯れ葉が　冬には雪が　頭上に降りつもるが
無言のまま　みじろぎもしない
幼い日　私は赤い南天の実を彼の目の中に入れ
身体の上に乗ってよく遊んだ
家族の誰かが　1日に一度しか訪れない
別宅の君主として　風雪に耐えながら見守ってきてくれた
時々　遊びに来る友人たちは縁側から　彼の絵を描いたり
写真も何枚も撮った　みんなは庭に彼が座っているだけで
心が和んでいるのだった

私が嫁いだ次の日　父は玄関で倒れ　病の床についたまま
8年の長い歳月が流れていった
本宅と西の家の主人である父を　ライオンが　かみ殺す
という理由で　恐れられ　彼は去っていった
それから　まもなく父が亡くなり　江戸時代からの
西の家も取り壊され　跡地には　兄たちの家が2軒建った

　　　ライオンは今　奈良行き近鉄電車　額田駅にある
　　　広いお屋敷の庭で　身体を休めていると聞く
　　　ああ　もう一度　銀色に冷たく光る
　　　王者の胴体に　私を乗せておくれ！

At An Oxford Gala Dinner

At a gala dinner while at the University,
I asked you,
"Can I open this envelope?"
To which you answered,
"Okay, you'll open it sometime anyway."
And I added,
"Yes. Just like life."

"And what is the meaning of life?"
Not the easiest question you could have chosen.
And staring at the surface of my wine glass,
I responded with,
"Maybe to make memories that ripple."
And you applauded me with the compliment,
"What a lovely answer."

Then you asked again,
"What is the meaning of life?"
As you mixed your ice cream with a cocktail spoon,
And the melting ice cream suddenly slipped down the spoon,
And with that you answered,
"This is the meaning of life."

オックスフォード大学のガラディナーで

船曳秀隆

オックスフォード大学に留学中のガラディナーで
「この封筒、開けていい？」
僕が君に聞くと
「いいよ。いずれ開けるんだから」
と君は答え
「そう、人生と一緒」
と僕は付け加えた

「人生の意味とは何か？」
なんて堅いことを君は僕に聞いてきて
ワイングラスの水面を見つめながら
「波紋のような思い出を作ることかな」
と答えると
「いい答えだ」
と拍手しつつ褒めてくれた

「人生の意味とは何か？」
なんて質問をまた君は僕に投げかけて
アイスクリームをマドラーで掻き混ぜる
ふいにスプーンから溶け落ちるアイスクリーム
最後に次のように答えた
「これが人生の意味だ」

Fake Living

In the room's vases
Fake flower arrangements that look real,
Hanging on the walls
Replicas of famous fake artists' work,
The hallway and living room floors
Have printed plywood flooring with fake wood colors,
On the walls
Fake tile wallpaper,
Curtains
Of flimsy fabric
Dyed with fake flowers and plants,
Our bags
Fakes made to look like famous brands,
Our clothes
The colors and patterns of fake brands,
Wallets
Filled with fake ten thousand-yen bills and credit cards,
And then people
Smiling fake smiles
Telling fake stories
And faking fondness,
Husbands and wives
Speak of fake love
Chat with fake smiles
Link arms and fake being loving couples,
Politicians
Talk about a fake future
And make fake promises.
It gets you down
Not knowing what is real and what is not.

似セ物の生活

船越貴穂

部屋の花瓶には
似セ物の花を本物の花のように飾り
壁に掛かっているのは
似セ物の有名画家らしき絵のコピー
廊下やリビングのフロアーは
偽セ物の木の色をしたプリント合版
壁に貼ってあるのは
似セ物のタイル柄のプリント紙
カーテンは
似セ物の花や草木を染めたような
ペラペラの布
持っているバッグは
似セ物のブランドのような作り物
着ている服は
偽セ物のブランドのような色と柄
財布の中身は
偽セ物の万札とカードがいっぱい
人々は
似セ者の笑顔を作り
似セ者の話をし
偽セ者の好意を示す
夫婦は
偽セ者の愛を語り
偽セ者の笑顔で話し
偽セ者の仲の良い夫婦で腕を組む
政治家は未来を語り
偽セ物の公約をする
ああ
偽セ物と本物との区別が付かなくなった

The Sunken World That Lies in The Pond by The Foot of The Mountain

Why, I wonder, do I have thoughts like this?
And past the reservoir where red winter grasses wave in the wind, a train runs by

A solitary fisherman bathed in faint late-winter sunlight
Enraptured in its gentle rays
Reflects on half a lifetime of struggle and lets the wind caress his cheeks
All day long he has been casting his line
The locals would have sunk their war wreckage and nuclear waste here
Where it waits deep down, linked to depths of the earth, still breathing, still
    in the hope of survival
Always alert for a chance to resurface
Deep down there the bones of the sacrificed weak are still whipped
War and terrorism still smolder
And the eyes of its youths are full of anger but reflect a sky full of stars
For they have not given up on the world

Behind these youths, people form lines
Climbing on and on towards the mountaintop
Climbing then sliding down again and, falling down, join hands
Then pant their way up again with all their bodily strength
        Towards a summit not so far out of reach
The power of the individual is small, but gathered is great
Never fear your insignificance, because resignation is extinction
Then the fisherman awoke in amazement, "Fish deep and bring up this
    sunken world"
A line of people were moving along the ridge, its black silhouette lined by
    the setting sun
The fisherman mumbled, "It's already dusk"
His raised his rod, with no bait nor hook at the end of its line
All he had caught out of the reddish-brown pond was a watery drop of illusion
Imagining a world not caught, and gazing at the surface of the pond
He got on his bicycle and made for home where his wife, spinning on a
loom, awaited his return

山裾の池に世界は沈んでいる

呉屋比呂志

「山裾の池に世界は沈んでいる」などとなぜ思うのだろう
野池のそばを　冬枯れの赤い草々が風にゆれ　横を電車が通ってゆく

釣り人一人　晩冬の薄い太陽に照らされ
その穏やかな日射に　うっとりとした気分で
闘い続けてきた半生を振り返り　風に頬を撫でさせて
ひねもす　釣り糸を垂れている
里人の手で　池に沈められているはずの戦争の残滓や核のゴミは
池の底につながる地球の深部で　息を止めず生き残りをかけて
浮き上がる機会を絶えず窺いつづけている
戦争・テロはくすぶって燃え続けている
青年たちの瞳は怒りに満ちているが　満点の星を映して輝く
青年たちは世界を諦めてはいない

その青年たちに続いて人々も列をつくり
山頂を目指してのぼりつづける
登っては滑り落ち　落ちては手をつなぎ合っては
登り続ける　息を弾ませ全身を使って
　　そんなに遠くない山頂へ
一人の力は小さいが　しかしあつまれば大きい
自己の小ささを恐れない　諦めは滅亡を意味するから
「池の中の世界を釣り上げ」驚いて目覚めた釣り人
稜線を行く人の列を　逆行が映し出し黒々と浮かびあがらせる
「はや夕暮れか」つぶやいた釣り人
上げた竿　釣り糸の先に釣り針もエサも無く
茶褐色の池から釣り上げたのは妄想の水滴一つ
釣り損ねた世界を思い　池の面を眺めて
機を織る妻の待つ我が家へと自転車のペダルを踏む

Spring Sigh

Joue-joue, the jaybirds sing,
And under the fern amongst the trees,
Where the sun shines through narrow gaps,
Yawning as if asleep,
Ladybirds all hunched up.

The field is full of buttercups,
From the hilltop,
Their golden carpet stretches out,
And with the urge to dive in
I looked up at the midday spring sky.

The sea is calm round the isle before me,
And the sun is high above the ocean blue,
Where the siren of a foreign ship echoes,
And in the offing the glitter of seagulls,
Somersaulting in a white stream.

I take in their fond, familiar scent,
And the sweet scent of flowing, verdant locks,
Then, reluctant to leave this fragrant world,
I sketch you on my canvas,
With foul tears trailing down.

When we cuddled close together on that hill,
The ridge of your breast
Gleamed with the sunlight pouring down on it;
I touched you timidly on your shoulders,
But alas, never knew your lips.

春の溜息

カケスは歌ふ　ジュウェジュウェと
木々の間の羊歯の下
狭き隙より陽は照れり
眠るやうなるあくびせし
天道虫はちぢくめり

お花畑はキンポウゲ
丘の上より眺めたり
黄金の絨毯拡がりて
飛び込みたがる心地して
空を見上げし春の昼

向かひの小島　波静か
青海原に日は高し
外国船の汽笛せり
沖に光るは鴎鳥
白く流れて宙返り

潮の匂ひを懐かしむ
緑の髪はかぐはしき
残り多しき香りにて
汝を絵取るキャンバスに
ヴィルとしたたる涙あり

丘の上にて添ひ付けば
汝が胸の稜線は
陽に照りをりて輝けり
肩に触れたり　ハジハジと
されど　汝が唇はつひに知らざり

Rambling

Sometimes the roaring sea shows itself
And sometimes it is a sea of calm
And mystery and outstanding beauty

A pearl that shines even in the night dark

Words of stone
Health, innocence, wealth
The smallest pearl is modest luck
While the pearl that amazes the eye
Cravingly sings an ode to life

And glitters on a lady's decolletage

The way forward and the way back so full of thorns
That not even the single ones you planted in my palm
At pearl and golden anniversaries
Gave me sufficient strength for it all

Long days are piling up one after another
So, for the happiness of shared understanding
Whisper me just once
Some word of thanks
For that is all I ask
In tears to God

そぞろ歩き

平野鈴子

とどろく海のときもある
凪の海のときもある
神秘さと卓越した美しさ
闇夜でさえ輝きをはなつ珠
石言葉は
健康・純粋無垢・富
ミニマムな粒はささやかな福運
目をみはる大きな粒は
むさぼるように人生を謳歌する
淑女のデコルテを目映いほどに煌めかせて
進むも戻るもいばらの道
真珠婚も金婚も
一粒のパールを掌に引きつけることさえ
私には力が備わっていなかった
つみ重ねたながい日
わかちあう幸せのために
きかせてよ
せめてねぎらいのことばを
ただそれだけでいい
神さまの涙に

Book

I still have the book I borrowed,
And, though I should return it,
Please lend it to me
Just a little longer.

Your conscientious letter came
To my new address after moving;
But since then, no word from you,
And I do not recall whether I answered or not.

Many years after,
I heard you had passed away;
Or, more exactly,
You were long since dead.

Then, amongst my old letters, I found yours;
I tried to recall the borrowed book,
But not even the title came to mind;
Instead, poems you penned come vividly back.

Sunglasses carelessly dropped in the sea,
Swaying downwards towards the seabed,
And finally are gone.

Your face distorted through those shades —
Did those dropping sunglasses
Finally reach you?

Between you and I,
Even now,
Book leaves are quietly turning.

本

　　本をお借りしたままです
　　お返ししないといけないのですが
　　もうしばらく
　　貸してください

わたしの引っ越し先に
そんな手紙をよこした律儀なきみ
それから便りもなく
わたしも返事を書いたかどうか

それから何年もして
きみが死んだことを
正確には
きみが死んでいたことを知った

古い手紙の中にきみの手紙を見つけた
どんな本を貸していたのか
本の名前も思い出せないのに
きみの詩がよみがえる

　　　海に落としてしまったサングラス
　　　揺れながら　海の底に落ちてゆき
　　　見えなくなった

サングラスの向こうのきみの顔がゆがむ
落ちていったサングラスは
きみにたどり着いただろうか

わたしときみの間には
今も本があり
静かにページが繰られてゆく

In The Fragrance

May roses
Pushing open

Petal upon petal
And amidst the petals
And yet further in

A flower beetle
A flower beetle

Smeared all over
With golden pollen
Sucking rose nectar

No human can ever do this
Not ever

All I can do
Is to pick the fallen petals
Still fragrant

And slip them softly
So they float in my bath

かおりのなかで

井上良子

ひらきはじめた
五月のバラ

かさねる　かさなる
はなびらのなかの
そのなかに

はなむぐり
はなむぐり

きんいろの
かふんにまみれて
みつをすう

ひとには　けっして
できないことなのよ

わたしはせめて
おちてもかおる
はなびらひろい

ゆぶねに　そっと
うかばせましょう

That Time, That Day

A midsummer grove just before noon
The buzz of cicadas enveloping all
And sinking deeply down
To memories lodged in the heart

The crowded station building
Cicadas in chorus mingling with the bustle
Strangely seeming to
Soothe our fatigue

Even face up close, I cannot hear the soft voices
Our train is ready to leave
A man wearing a broad red sash
Leans out of the train window

A young mother holds out a babe deep asleep
And a man, smiling, pokes its cheek
Whispers a word or two
Before closing his window

The train moves off
Passengers waving quietly through windows
To people waving small flags, bidding farewell
As time passes ruthlessly on

Then a blinding flash of light and immense roar
Burns the station and all in it to dust

And with it all the feelings of love of all living things

あの日あの時

真夏の　昼前の木立を
ミンミンとおおいつくす　セミの声
ミンミンと　こころの奥底へ
忘れ得ぬ　思い出へと

ごった返す駅舎
雑踏とまじりあうセミの声は
疲れたひとびとを　励ますかのよう
いつもにはなく……

顔を近づけても　やさしい声が聞きとれない
出発ま近の列車
はば広の赤いたすきをかけた男が
車窓から身を乗り出す

眠りつづける赤んぼ　さし出す若い母親
男は　笑いながら赤んぼのほっぺたをつつくと
ひと言二言　ささやいて
車窓を閉じる

動き出す列車
しずかに手を振る　車窓のひと
小旗をふりながら　別れを告げる人々に
時が　無慈悲に刻まれてゆく

鮮烈な光と轟音が
駅舎も人々をも　焼きはらった

生きとしいけるものの　愛の心までも

Ta

Not a drop of saliva, no utterance of any sort —
Does the brain signal the morning; and the morning signal the brain?
First, the old woman tries to bend her ten toes;
Then she gets up, turns over the duvet,
Takes a deep breath,
And rubs her hands to invite the maze of blue veins into the
    labyrinth.
Invoking the *Namu Kanzeon Bosatsu*, she chants *Namu Namu Na**
    over and over,
Until her lungs have exhausted their single big breath.
Her tongue, rounded and dry, makes a rusty squeak but will not move,
Like a machine that has run out of oil.
Now not even the right side of her upper lip sings,
Or, even if she tries, breath alone exhales and exhales again.

A drop of dripping water, illusion turning it into a flush of red air —
In the market fresh quenching food and drinks,
Lined up in great piles,
Remain cut off;
A rustic brick house blown away and turned to rubble,
Born in that rubble corner,
In its mud-clad clothing,
A bunch of tearful notes,
Drops of a voice,
Cut off;
A babe opens a doll's eyes and looks at it —
The family scattered — the townsfolk and livestock, too.

Not even the H of Help
Not even the *Ta* of *Tasukete* form on our lips.

    * Buddhist chant

TA

加藤千香子

一滴の唾なければ　声は出ない
脳が朝を知らせるのか　朝が脳に合図するのか
先づ　足の 10 本の指は無事か　曲げてみる
年寄りは起き上がる　羽根ぶとんめくり
深呼吸して
青い血管を迷宮に誘う手をこすり合わせ
南無観世音菩薩　一息の續くかぎり
唱えている　南無南無　南
舌が乾いてまるまり　きしんで　動かない
油切れ機械だ
右側の上唇も　うたにならない
うたおうとしても　吐く息が　吐く息が

したたる一滴の水　幻想は赤い風になる
青果市場にずらっと山積みされていた
みずみずしい　たべもの　のみもの
絶たれたまま
爆風に飛ばされ　瓦礫となった日干し煉瓦の家
その隅に産み落とされ
泥衣裳着て
もう泣く涙の音符の一つぶ
声のしずく
ぷつん　と　きれた
赤ん坊は人形の目を　見開いて　見ている
一家離散していった　住民　家畜たち

タスケテ
TAが　出ない

In The Season When Light And Dark Intersect
— For My Dear Friend, Anne Frank

I learned that you passed away in February
In your dark, shadowed house where you never ceased gazing at
the light

I cannot recall when you first visited
But it was like finding an elder sister
Later you turned to friend
And then a younger sister
Finally, before I knew it, you had become my daughter
And it was then that I first visited that dark, shadowed house

It stood on a canal not far from the station
And going up the steps one by one…
I found a small girl staring at the light
From a small window

The more confined the broader your dream
As it slipped from your small window
And spread further and further into the sky

Now long after
Those great wings still beat
The liberty you craved
Is yours now
Circling forever
Through the hearts of all the world

And your day of remembrance is in the season
When light intersects with the darkness
And though we do not know the actual day
It will never be forgotten

光と陰が交差する季節に
── 親愛なるアンネフランクへ

河合真規子

２月があなたの命日月と知った
陰の家から光を見続けていたあなた

あなたはいつ私の前に現れたのだろう
初めての時　あなたは姉のようだった
そして　あなたは友となる
やがて　あなたは妹になり
いつのまにか娘になった
その頃初めて陰の家を訪ねた

駅からもそう遠くない運河沿いのその家
その階段を一歩ずつ…
小さな窓から光を見続けている少女が
そこにいた

束縛されるほど　夢は膨らむ
あの小さな窓をすり抜けて
どんどん広がる夢

遥かな今
あなたの夢は大きく羽ばたいて
あなたが切望した自由は
今あなたものとなり
世界中を　人々の心の中を
永遠に駆け巡る

命日月は光と陰が交差する季節
しかし命日もわかっていないひとりの少女が
もう忘れられることはない

Despair

This walking
Started with cheers at a few toddling steps
But those days of joy are soon gone

Endlessly
We walk on and on
For to be human is to be full of sorrow
And blind to the end

And if I am born into this fated lot
At least I should try
To enjoy the world
In which I have found
A reason to live

Such happiness and joy
As if my eyes and tongue had popped out
But tiring of those happy days
The aftermath brought

The oblivion of memory

And then...
A woman walking
A man walking

On and on
Without end
All of us
Piling up our sadness

絶望

歩みは
ヨチヨチの歓声で始まった
喜びの日々は飛んでゆく

どこまでも
歩いて・歩いて
人は悲しいものだ
果ては見えない

生まれてきたからには
この世を
楽しまなければ損だ
見つけた
生きがい

楽しくて嬉しくて
目玉も舌も飛び出した
楽しみ疲れたそのあとに
やって来るものは

忘却

そして
女が歩く
男が歩く

どこまでも・どこまでも
歩き続けて
人は
悲しみを積み上げていく

From Afar

Occasionally, even now,
They say you can hear the sigh of the universe*
And though I've never been to Death Valley,
When I read that, I felt a reverberation reviving my skin.

Engrossed in conversation with a friend,
A moment occurs when the face suddenly becomes that of a stranger;
Or you wake up in the middle of the night, and feel it is not your room —
That moment when you do not know where you are;
There is always something that echoes behind your temples
And everything blends into its reverberation.

If you look up from the bottom of a deep well,
They say you can see the stars even in the daytime;
But if you lose sight of yourself in the world of reality,
What is it that you see then?

Then one morning as I was thinking about such things,
My face, pasted there in the mirror,
Seemed about to peel off;
Hurriedly putting my hand to it,
I feel the same unevenness as always.
Yet, in the mirror, I wear the same troubled expression —
The part around my chin starting to peel away,
And regardless of my confusion,
The face of the mirror continues to peel.
And when it falls completely off,
A woman in a Noh mask stands there,
Staring at me unflinchingly.

* The background noise that is said to be the sound that occurred when the
universe was created.

遠くから

北口汀子

デス・バレーでは今も時折
*宇宙の溜息が聴こえると言う
私はデス・バレーに行ったことは無いが
その話をどこかで読んだとき肌に蘇ってくる残響を感じた

友達と喋るのに夢中になりながら
不意に相手の顔が見知らぬ他人となってしまう刹那
夜中に目醒めたとき自分の部屋の空気に違和感を覚え
そこが何処なのかわからなくなってしまう刹那
決まってこめかみの奥に鳴り響くものがあり
その残響の中に全てが溶け込んでいく

深い井戸の底から覗けば
昼でも星が見えると言う
現実の中で自分を見失ったら
いったい何が見えてくるのだろう

そんなことを思っていたある朝
鏡の面に張り付いている私の顔が
剥がれそうになっていた
慌てて顔に手をやれば
いつもと変わらぬ凸凹に触れたが
鏡の中の私は困ったような表情を浮かべたまま
顎の辺りがペランと剥がれかけている
戸惑っている私にお構いなく
鏡の顔は剥がれている
すっかり剥がれ落ちた後には
能面を付けた女がじっと
こちらを見詰めているばかりだ

　＊宇宙創生時に生じたとされるバックグラウンドノイズ

To Boris Karloff And Peter Cushing

Like a steam locomotive,
Towing its passenger carriages,
I know that everybody will descend and go their way sooner or later,
As I connect them to their mortal fates pulling them onwards down
    the tracks.
From broken coaches, they will break away one by one,
And crying their death throes, fall to the bottom of the gorge.

For hundreds and thousands of years, I run on and on without end,
For I am a bloodsucker, a vampire.
A monster that never dies, and can never be destroyed.
I turn my cape quickly round,
And with my one lantern, pursue again, no doubt, the black night rails.

"No," you say. "You are always dead."

Dead, yet unable to grasp the meaning of doom,
A worthless doll made of clod.
A paranoid count and his sweetheart
— his mask slipping away in the long, cursed rain;
A good soup, you ask? A good soup is made of young, virgin blood.
Oh, life is splendid! The shining red *al dente* of this Bolognese
    sauce!

Today again, I salivate over a maiden's white neck,
For I am, first and foremost, a cursed thing,
Envying the sunlight.

I will return to dust,
And the locomotive go on again,
With just an old, dead fireman on the footplate.

ボリス・カーロフとピーター・カッシングに。

北村こう

ぼくは蒸気機関車のように、
あとの客車を引っ張って走っているんだ
いずれみんないなくなることはわかっていて
致死の運命たちを連結したまま、鉄路の上を、走るんだ
こわれた客車から順に連結ははずれ —— 断末魔をあげながら
谷底へ堕ちていくだろう

数百年、数千年　ぼくはどこまで走って行ける
吸血鬼だから、バンバイアだから。
怪物はいつでも死なない、壊れない。
バッとマントをひるがえし
見えない夜のレールの上を　ランタンひとつで　行くだろう

「違うでしょ」と、君は言う「あなたはずっと死んでるの」

死んでいながら、死の意味をはかりかねている
土塊でできたつまらない人形
妄想狂の伯爵とその恋人 —— 長雨が祟って仮面がずれたのか
うまいスープはなんだ？　処女の純血である
生命はすばらしい！　あかく照るミートソースは
　実に歯ごたえがある！

ふたたび、白い少女の首にたらりと体液をこぼし
ぼくは第一、憑りつかれているんだと
あの陽光をうらやんだ。

ぼくは土に還り
蒸気機関車は未だ走るけれども
乗っているのはただ　死せる年老いた機関手だ

Silence

Enter through the narrow gate
For wide is the gate and broad is the road
That leads to destruction,
And many enter through it.

Have I entered through the narrow gate?
Am I trying to enter that narrow gate?

I am finally close to my eighties —
Those I can call friends have departed one by one,
And now I walk lonely and alone.

The way onwards is painted with only one color —
The color of anxiety.

The heavens are covered with clouds and the thunder roars —
Anxiety, hesitation and the cold rain of despair
Lash cruelly down on me.

My God, My God, why hast thou forsaken me?
I thought I heard someone call

I thought I tried to call to that same call

Lord God, have I entered through your narrow gate?
Am I trying to enter your narrow gate?

But the silence alone
Continues.

沈黙

清沢桂太郎

　狭き門より入れ
　滅びにいたる門は大きく　その路は廣く
　之より入る者おほし

私は狭き門より入ったのであろうか
私は狭き門より入ろうとしているのであろうか

齢はとうに八十路に近く
友とすべき者は一人二人と去り
今は一人孤独に歩んでいる

行くべき先は不安色一色で
塗りつぶされている

天は雲で覆われ雷鳴が轟き
不安と迷いと冷たい絶望の雨が
激しく私に降りかかってくる

　わが神わが神　なんぞ我を見棄て給ひし
私は誰かの叫びを聞いたようだ
私は誰かの叫びを叫ぼうとしたようだ

　神よ　私は狭き門より入ったのでしょうか
　私は狭き門より入ろうとしているのでしょうか

沈黙のみが
続いている

Whale Alice

An animal odor spouts from her fumaroles
As the smokey blast of brine soars upwards
Her nasal cavity is like that of an elephant
As this inhabitant of the water hemisphere
Raises her smokey waterfall signal
Her base in the world of fish
She swims the seas scattering her briny breath
High into the sky as she eases through the rough

     Her huge mass the size of the Super Computer Kei

She manipulates oceans at her will
While the hunters hide, never missing the moment of capture

Whale Song 51.75 Hz

This unique frequency
Is particular in the animal world as well
One scholar has said it is
"Like a Matryoshka doll made of wooden blocks
  Or the voices of children as they run around
  It stimulates the academic imagination"
It echoes off islands in an ocean without signposts
And soothes with its smooth SEA SONG
Is she playing alone on some distant horizon
Fated never to sing or mate for the rest of her life?

Ah, Alice, the humpback whale — lonely and proud

Whale・アリス

久保俊彦

噴火孔からの獣臭
水煙を囂々とあげ
鼻腔は象のようだ
水半球の生息域に
滝の狼煙をあげる
塩基は魚類の領域
空にばらまきながら泳いでいる
荒れた中で呼吸は容易いようだ

　　　京ほどの大きな塊

自由自在に海を操っているように見える
狩人は隠れて捕獲の瞬間を見逃さないが

鯨の歌・51.75Hz

この特異な周波数は
動物界でも特異な音
ある学者は表現した
「組木細工のマトリョーシカ
　子が遊び運動する声と似て
　学術的想像力を刺激させる」
標識がない大海原の洋島にも響く
なめらかな SEA SONG に癒される
遥か彼方で遊んでいるのだろうか
天涯孤独歌唱交配を全くしない

孤高な Humpback Whale・アリス！

When I Was A Precocious Child

MAKITA Hisami

As a precocious child
I had this queer habit
Of popping new words into my mind
One after another like throwing pills

It feels nostalgic now and
A bit embarrassing
But I was hoping for some special effect

Sadly though
The stomached pills never dissolved
And all my seasonal letters died in the post

In my precocious playground
Red flowers bloomed at the grave I made with friends

A bitter sweet gift of the gods
Were the word plays I could never solve
On my way home in the evening glow

Then as I was entering the adult world
Something dropped into my morning postbox with a faint sound
Fresh warm words
Like they were still in the sender's mind

The premonition of a disease named adult
For which I have not yet found a prescription

I placed them on the altar of my heart

And from that day on
Words turned to prayers of celebration

私が大人びた子供だった頃

牧田久未

私が大人びた子供だった頃
私は適度に病んでいた
言葉などという錠剤を
ポンポン心に放り込んでいた

懐かしいけど
恥ずかしい
この薬の独自の効き目を期待した

けれど
胃の中の錠剤はいつまでも溶けず
真夜中のポストでは季節の手紙が死んでいく

大人びた子供の遊び場
幼なじみと作ったお墓に赤い花が咲く

神様の御褒美は甘くて苦い
夕焼けの帰り道
いつまでもとけない言葉遊び

大人になろうとする頃
朝のポストでコトリと音がした
さっきまで心に張り付いていたような
生温かい言葉

大人という病の予感
効き目のある処方箋はまだ見つからない

私はそれを祭壇に捧げた

その日から
言葉は長い祝詞になった

Bathing Care

I am having the toes of my right foot washed
By a nurse who
Was a complete stranger until yesterday.

After I get out of the bath,
She takes out a little toolbox and
Trims the toenails of my right foot,
Which I cannot cut myself,
Skillfully managing all her tools —
The nail clippers, files, a sonde* and others —
Carefully and tenderly.

And into the bargain,
She clears a corn that is being treated
With her tweezers.

Once a week, on the day she visits,
I reveal my true, naked self,

Nothing, not even the private parts, hidden,
And sometimes, I split my sides laughing.

To this unpretentious nurse who is just herself,
And protected by her human touch,
I entrust my whole being.

* A tool for removing the unwanted matter between the nail and the skin.

入浴介護

三浦千賀子

昨日まで全く知らなかった
看護師さんに
右足先を洗ってもらっている

風呂上がりには
小さな道具箱を出して
自分では切れない
右足の爪を切ってくれる
ニッパーや、やすりや
爪切りやゾンデ*
等の道具を駆使して
やさしくていねいに

おまけに
治療中の魚の目の後始末も
ピンセットなどで処理してくれる

週一回のその日
恥ずかしいところも隠さずに

素の自分をさらけ出している私
ときにお腹がよじれるぐらい笑ったり

飾りけなく自然体の看護師さん
その人間味に守られて
すべてをゆだねています

　　　＊爪と皮膚の間のほこりなどを取る道具

Poppies

As I make my way down the slope, I see some poppies blooming from a gap in the asphalt right next to the garbage collection area. I wonder why I have not noticed them on my daily walk before now. Two four-petaled flowers in shades of purple swaying in the breeze. A miracle that no one picked them before they bloomed.

The poppy is also called the Beautiful Lady Yu, after the favorite concubine of Xiang Yu, the King of Chu. In 202 B.C., when he was surrounded and realized he had been defeated at the Battle of Gaixia, he composed this farewell poem: "Ah, Yu, my Yu. What will your fate be?" It is said that the poppy grew from the blood of his beloved as she took her own life.

About sixty centimeters tall, and bathed in the early summer sun, their stems and leaves are covered in thick, coarse hair. Every day since, I have stopped to look at them. And there, as if to prompt my imagination, after the petals have fallen, the robust seed pods rigidly fixed to their stalks.

芥子の花

水野ひかる

　坂を下ると、ごみ収集場のすぐ傍らのアスファルトの隙間に、芥子の花が咲いている。散歩をしているのに、何故見過ごしていたのだろう。紫の濃淡の絞りの四弁花が二つ風に揺れている。花が咲くまで誰にも抜かれなかったのは、奇蹟である。

　この花は、虞美人草とも呼ばれる。虞美人とは、中国の楚の王項羽の寵姫のことである。紀元前二百二年、垓下に包囲された項羽が敗戦を悟ったとき、〈虞や虞やなんじをいかにせん〉と辞世の詩を詠んだ。それほどまでに愛された虞美人が命を絶ったとき、その血から生えてきたという芥子の花。

　六十センチほどの丈の花は、初夏の日差しを浴びて、茎や葉に粗い毛が密生している。その日から毎日、立ち止まっては眺めている。そこには、思いを巡らせるよう、花びらが散った跡に、しっかりと実が結ばれている。

Your Eyes

Those eyes of ebony
Great, round eyes of black light
Eyes too strangely beautiful
To be human

No ornament
No black crystal, black coral, black glass, black marble
Can rival their dark depths
And what, I wonder, do they reflect?

Some human form or the world itself
Cleansed of all impurity
Forgive — ordinary beings
Do not always possess such clarity

And in the morning I will come to you
Even if the Genkai Sea should be wild
And the storm hounds me
To reflect pure and beautiful in your eyes

To that end
I will hold your beauty tightly to me
And to that end
The earth will spin in reverse

Just for that short hour

あなたの瞳

水崎野里子

あなたの黒い瞳
まん丸でピカピカ光ってる
不思議なの　人間がこんなにきれいな瞳
持っているなんて

黒水晶　黒珊瑚　黒硝子　黒大理石
どんな作り物も
あなたには　かなわない
あなたの瞳は何を映すの？

きっと汚さを外した
人間の姿　世界の姿
ごめんね　人間は　いつでも
そんなに澄んではいなかった

明日　あなたに会いに行く
玄界灘が　荒れても
颱風が　追いかけて来ても
きれいな人間を　あなたの瞳に映したい

そのために
きれいなあなたを抱きしめる
そのために
地球が逆に廻る

その時間のために

Cicada Chorus

— so that, a decade on, the triple distress of
the Great East Japan Earthquake is not forgotten

March 11, 2011 — the massive earthquake and tsunami
Took the lives of over twenty thousand,
And the mourners will outnumber them many times over.

Then, as if to attack the survivors
Even further,
The great explosion of the Fukushima Nuclear Power Plant
Poured radiation down upon them —
On scenes from which I would avert my eyes, and
On unchanged everyday life —
Invisible radioactive rays pouring down.

Rivers and oceans, plants and cows, water and soil,
Since then, all has changed.
On the ground, water is said to be the only thing that cicadas take,
And that water is now contaminated.

Awaking earlier than usual, the *higurashi*
Would have felt the terrible tremble of the ground;
And possibly,
Like us, they sensed
They may not have long to live.

The *higurashi* chirp as if their time is dear,
Echoing
As if they were coupling this world to the other.

And if radioactivity had a sound,
It would be like an insane chorus of cicadas,
That could not fail to reach these ears.

蟬時雨
せみしぐれ

—— 十年が経つ東日本大震災の三重苦の記憶を
風化させないために ——

2011年3月11日の大地震と大津波は
2万人余の命を奪っていった
亡くなった者を悼む人はその何倍にもなるだろう

追い討ちをかけるように
生き残った人々の上に
福島原子力発電所の大爆発で
放射線が降り注いだ
目を被いたくなる光影や
変わらない日常にも
目に見えない放射線が降り注ぐ

川も海も　草も牛も　土も水も
あれ以来　全てが変わってしまった
地上では　水しか飲まないと言われる蟬
その水も　放射能におかされていると言う

いつもより早く　ひぐらしが目覚めたのは
大地の強い揺れを感じたからだろう
もしかすると
人も蟬と同じように　わずかな命しか
残されていないのかもしれない

時を惜しむように　ひぐらしが鳴いている
その声は
あの世とこの世を結ぶかのように続く

もしも　放射能に音があるのならば
蟬時雨のような狂った声が
この耳に　届くにちがいない

Tree Sounds

kokkototo   tonto~n
Like a woodpecker
Let your tree sound resonate

tsura~tsu~tsu   tsura tsura
Where is it flowing from?
The colour of blood or the colour of flame

kira~   chirari~   chika
Let me see your light
Like from a lighthouse

And dance
In the amusement park of words
In the forest of tree sound
Like your reflection in a mirror

樹　音

森　ちふく

コッコットト　トントーン
きつつきのように
あなたの　樹音を　響かせて下さい

ツラーツーツー　ツラツラ
流れてくる　どこから？
血の色　それとも　焔色

キラー　チラリー　チカ
視せて下さい
燈台のような光を

舞って下さい
ことばの　遊園地で
樹音という森で
鏡が　反射するように

Sky

For long I used to think
The sky was
To be looked up at

Though ah —
If the earth were transparent
Through its crystal ball
Would be endless star after star after star

Under our very feet
Is a sky full of stars
Spread before our eyes

そら

森木　林

ずっと　思いこんでいた
そら　は
見上げるものだ　と

けれど　あぁ
もしも　大地が　透きとおったなら
水晶玉の　むこうには
果てしない　星　星　星　……

ぼくらの　足もとには
いつも　星ぞらが
ひろがっている

MORITA Yoshiko

That Star-spangled Night

Even now, the recurring ravages of war under the name of justice —
Then suddenly I recall the starry sky of home in Okinawa, and wonder how
The lovely blue-eyed, blonde-haired George, two, and Robert, four, are
    doing now.

The small send-off party for John going to service in the War in Vietnam —
The two kids held in his lap, one then the other and romping around;
His wife interpreted, with the laughter embracing us all, helping us forget
    the occasion;
Then, after firm parting handshakes, we prayed silently to a sky outside
    full of stars.

At the Kadena Air Base, John hugged his wife and children, and would
    not let them go.
I'll be back! And we'll be waiting for you!
Words without voice pressed in the hearts of those seeing him off;
And John kneeling down and kissing the runway before he flew away.

He's back! John is back! Everybody united in their relief —
But John, who had survived the fires of war, was no longer John.
As if he believed his beloved wife was Vietnamese, with unbearable
    violence, and barbaric, drunken behavior,
John's suffering became, in equal measure, the suffering of his wife.
Every time she was exposed to the brink, she had no choice but to disappear.
Left there, he took George on his shoulders, and Robert by the hand,
And passed my house with his large trunk, to the house of his in-laws,
An exhausted shell, his back climbing the slope.

Daddy, don't go! Daddy! Dad! Don't go! Don't go!
Infant pleas sucked into the star-spangled night.

More than a half century has passed, yet that whole scene is still engraved there
The cries of those two little boys, and me living with their screams.

満点の星空

森田好子

正義の名のもと今なお繰り返される戦禍
ふと甦る故郷沖縄の星空　今ごろどうしているのだろうか
ブルーアイ　金髪の愛くるしい２才のジョージと４才のロバート

ベトナム戦争に出向くジョンのためのささやかな壮行会
ジョージもロバートも次々と膝に抱かれてはしゃぎまわっている
妻の通訳もありその場は出兵を忘れさす笑い声で包まれていた
固い握手を交わし外に出ると満点の星空　誰もが静かに祈っていた

嘉手納基地では妻を子どもを抱きしめたまま離そうとしないジョン
きっと帰ってくる！　ここで待っているから！
言葉にならない言葉は見送る人たちの心の中にも迫ってくる
ジョンは滑走路に跪き口づけをした後　飛び立った

帰ってきたよ　ジョンが帰ってきた　みんな胸を撫で下ろした
しかし、戦火を潜って生還した彼は別人になっていた
最愛の妻がベトナム人に見えるのか耐え難いDV　蛮行　酒乱
ジョンの苦しみはそのまま妻の苦しみになっていった
命の危機にさらされるたび　妻は姿を消すほかなかった
残されたジョンはジョージを肩車に　ロバートの手をひき
大きなトランクを持ち私の家の前を歩いて妻の実家へ
憔悴しきったジョンの背中が坂道をのぼっていく

パパー　Don't go !　パパー！パパー！　Don't go !　Don't go !
幼い二人の叫び声は満点の星空にスイコマレルように消えていった

あれから半世紀余り　全ての光景があの日のまま刻まれている
幼い二人の叫び声と共に　今も私は　生きているのだ

Flying Fish

When I went into the Maeda's house, I turned and, in the darkness,
Found lots of triangular fins stuck to the back of their sliding
   wooden door.
Misses, what are these?
Flying fish! Have you never heard of them?
Do they fly?
Fish?
Sure they do —
Flying fins swimming along the door's wooden grain.

The bloke in the fishmonger's
Sometimes puts fish into big boxes attached to his bicycle and
   does the rounds.
Where's your mom?
Tell her the fishmonger's here.
Mackerel, sardines and horse mackerel lying in chipped ice,
When he gets to my house, most of the fish have been sold.
Horse mackerel with big white eyes,
Sardines with their head plunged into a box with little ice.
But I never saw a live flying fish.
His round is over after he goes two houses on, I think,
Before he speeds down the slope and home.

At the well, mom splits the belly of the mackerel open,
And, after sprinkling it with salt, she returns to her work in the field.
I look at it through the fish screen,
I have been told not to touch it, but am tempted;
Its flabby, white body has none of the blue of a flying fish,
The fins are short and not pointed in a triangle —
Not easy for it to fly away and escape.

And this is why you were caught,
I tell the mackerel politely.

飛びうお

前田さんの家にいくと
振り返った板戸の暗がりに三角のヒレが何枚も貼ってある
おばちゃんこれ何
飛びうおだが知らんか？
飛ぶんか？
魚が？
そう
板の木目に乗って泳ぐ飛びうおのヒレ

魚屋のおっちゃんが
時々自転車のごっつい荷台に乗せて売りに来る
お母ちゃんおんならんか
魚屋が来たって呼んできてごせや
氷に混じってサバ、イワシ、アジがばらっと寝ている
我が家の前に来るときは大方が売れて
アジは白目をむいて
イワシは少ない氷に頭を突っ込んでいる
生きた飛びうおなんて見たことない
もう二軒奥へ行くとしまいだな
おっちゃんは坂道を自転車をすっ飛ばして帰る

母ちゃんは井戸端で買ったサバの腹を裂き
塩を振って畑に戻る
私は魚の網戸に入っているのを見る
触るなと言われたけど触りたい
飛びうおの蒼いからだではなくダラリと太ったサバの体
ヒレは短く三角に尖っていない
飛んで逃げることは難しそうだ

こんなだから捕まるのだ
ていねいに言って聞かせる

Compassion in Autumn

So as not spread the coronavirus,
I do not return home;
The papers tell us mountain communities are already infected.

On top of the poverty of post-war defeat,
Tuberculosis, typhoid and dysentery came up the Yuragawa River,
Though children fishing its limpid stream were spared.

Nowadays kids are few —
They ride the school bus
To distant campuses.

The schoolhouse our grandparents were proud of lies vacant,
The cherry trees round the large playground are no doubt weeping;
And my sister, three years older, left her guilt and gratitude when
    she left home.

It conveys its warmth like a spring breeze —
Caring for parents, looking after the children,
Leaving the mark of love.

Touched by the dear fragrance of young rice stalks and the scent
    of straw,
My sister was given a bride's sendoff
With a procession and a trousseau.

Stars sparkle throughout the firmament —
The Milky Way pours onwards over the village,
Cleansing the earth of its anxieties,

Spreading its cosmic wonders in the palm of the sky,
And covering all in a veil of compassion.

秋の情け

コロナを持ち込んではいけないと
故郷へ帰らない
新聞は　すでに山間の町にも入っていると告げる

敗戦後の貧しさに乗じて　結核やチフス　赤痢が
由良川の上流まで　のぼってきたが
清流で魚捕りをする子供は大丈夫だった

今は　子どもが少ない
スクールバスに乗って
遠くの本校へ行く

祖父たちが誇りにした校舎は空いたまま
広い運動場の桜の木も涙しているだろう
３歳上の姉は　私に情けを残してくれた

情けは　春風のように温かみを伝える
父母を助け　子守りをし
愛情という姿を残す

稲の匂い　藁の匂い　哀しく
嫁ぐ姉の姿を　見送った
嫁入り道具とともにゆく行列を

天（そら）一面に星が輝く
天の川も　村の上を　とうとうと渡り
地上の憂いを吸い上げ

空の掌（たなごころ）に　宇宙の不思議を散らばせて
情けというベールを掛けている

My Hope

2021 is the Year of the Ox,
And taking my lead from this beast,
I made my New Year resolution,
Wrote "SLOWLY" in *sumi* ink, and put it in a frame.

I have aged and, lately, suffered serious illness,
So I can only do things slowly;
Each night, my head propped on my hand,
I look at the calligraphy in its frame.

As I gaze, the brush strokes' image deepens,
And I have come to think
How much better it would be
If only the whole of life could slow down.

If our leaders the world over would look
Beyond quick profit, power and hegemony;
And consider the future more seriously
For this planet and its children.

Today, as always, dawn has broken quietly in —
Everyone in the US, are you sleeping soundly?
Everyone in China, are you all well?
Won't you gather around our slow table and eat?

僕の願いごと

南条ひろし

2021 年（令和 3 年）の干支は、丑である
丑のふるまいに倣って
正月、今年 1 年の目標・方針として
「ゆっくり」と墨書し、額に入れた

僕は、歳もとり、最近大きな病気もした
何事も、ゆっくりとしかできなくなった
「ゆっくり」と書かれた額の文字を
毎夜、寝室で腕を枕に眺めている

眺めているうちに、「ゆっくり」のイメージが深まって
世の中全体が、もっとゆっくりとならないか
なればいいな　と
思うようになった

世界中の国々のリーダーには
目先の利益や権力、覇権に目を奪われず
地球や子供達の将来のこと　もっと
真剣に考えていただけないだろうか……

今日も静かに夜が明けてきた
アメリカの皆さんは、ぐっすり眠れていますか
中国の皆さんは、お変わりございませんか
食卓でも囲んで、少しゆっくりしませんか

Teru

Teru is a strong boy
Born on December 29th, 2020
One month earlier than he was due
His small, red body gave out his first big cry

Teru is a strong boy
With tummy full of his mother's milk
And supported in the bath tub on his father's great palms
He stretched out his limbs as far as they would go

Teru is a strong boy
Two days ago, at his four-month check-up
His weight had doubled since birth
And the doctor praised his progress

And yesterday when his mother laid him on his tummy on the bed
He supported himself with his arms and raised his head
Today he is crawling on all fours as if rowing with oars
The marvel of yesterday's impossible becoming possible the day after

Teru is a strong boy
Soon he will crawl, grasp something and stand
Stand up strongly all by himself
And then, after days of toddling, he will stride out upon his way

Teru is a strong boy
Without hesitation he shall overcome each unknown presented to him
He will move on and on with each step cleared
His lovely almond eyes wide open to the world

照くん

照くんは頑張り屋さん
2020年の12月29日に
予定日より1ヶ月も早く誕生した
小柄な身体を真っ赤にして　大きな大きな産声をあげた

照くんは頑張り屋さん
お母さんのたっぷりの母乳と
お父さんのがっちりした掌の入浴介助で
思い切り　浴槽の中で手足を伸ばした

照くんは頑張り屋さん
一昨日　4ヶ月検診で保健所を訪ねたら
体重が　誕生時の2倍になっていると
担当医に褒められた

照くんは頑張り屋さん
昨日　お母さんが照くんを俯せに寝かせたら
両腕で身体を支え　ウーンと頭を擡げることができた
今日はもう　オールを漕ぐ要領で匍匐前進をする
〜前日できなかったことが　翌日にはできる素晴らしさ〜

照くんは頑張り屋さん
間もなく　這い這いをして　掴まり立ちして
1人でしゃんと立ち上るだろう
ヨチヨチ歩きを終えたら　1人でしっかり歩き出す……

照くんは頑張り屋さん
次々と出現する未知の世界を　躊躇うことなく乗り越えて
前進して行くことだろう
切れ長の瞳を大きく見開いて

NISHIMOTO Megumi

Irresistible Feeling

A flowing vine
Floating amidst fresh greenery
Entangling itself, reaches upwards
And bursts open

It wears a coat
Of countless tiny blossoms
That bloom together
Like music

Its pulse
Like keys on a piano
Struck one after another
Beating blood on and on

Its smooth skin
Crawls slowly on
Tactile, never tiring
Of the constant bodily overlap

It throbs with the throbbing pulse of life
Until its gorgeous decay
Is delivered to its loved one
Even if it were over planetary distance

とめられない想い

流れる蔓が
新緑を浮かべて
からまり　昇り
弾ける

小さな花を
無数にまとい
奏でるように
咲いてしまう

鼓動が　打つ
鍵盤が連打される
叩き　叩きつけ
血を送り続ける

なめらかな肌を
這い　ゆっくりと
触れてゆく　あきることのない
重なる肉体の

命の躍動が打つ　打つ
華やかに朽ち果てるまで
想人に届ける
惑星距離であろうとも

The Film

The movie clearly finished with its ending caption
And with it, the man who died
And the woman who chased him
Yet the film goes on
With blurred body contours
Then the lights are turned on
And the man next to me
And the woman next to him
Both stand up, their arms crossed
Yet still
It goes on
And after leaving the cinema
I telephoned
To say: Goodbye
To whom?
Last night I had a dream of my soul crying out
Bitterly and without restraint
What on earth am I doing?
I asked myself, and took a cigarette
Did the man in the movie cry alone?
The actor did not cry
And so
Complaining like this to myself
I made my way home
Still angry
And my wife asked me
"How was today's movie?"
"I don't really know,
I wish someone would do something —
It just will not end."

フィルム

岡本光明

『完』は映画の終わり
死んでしまった男
追いかけた女
ぼやけた肉体の輪郭で
まだ　続いていく
明かりがつけられて
隣の男
その隣の女
腕を組んで立ち上がった
それでも
まだ　続いていく
映画館を出て
電話をかけた
さようなら　と
誰に？
昨夜　はらわたがちぎれるほど
思い切り泣いた夢を見た
俺は一体何をしているのだろう　と
たばこを一服
映画の男は人知れず泣いただろう
俳優は泣かなかった
だから
ぶつぶつ不平を言いながら
家に帰って
腹を立てていると
女房がやってきて
今日はどうだった？
どうもこうもないよ
何とかしてくれよ　もう
終わらないんだ

Snake

Blue spine
Slipping swiftly away
Into the grass

Though there is no road
You are already
A secret
Endless path

Though there is no river
You are already
The lonely murmur
Of an endless stream

Though there is no wind
As you slip between the grass
You are already
Invisible flute flutter

Though the sun has set
Stretching endlessly
Beyond the sea of grass
You are already
The blue-white mountain ridge

蛇

草むらへ
あわてて逃げてゆく
青い背骨よ

道はなくとも
すでにお前は
どこまでも続いてゆく
ひそやかな小道

川はなくとも
すでにお前は
どこまでも流れてゆく
寂しいせせらぎ

風はなくとも
すでにお前は
草に分け入る
姿なき笛の音

陽は落ちても
すでにお前は
草の海のかなた
果てしなく続く
青白き山脈

Mother And Daughter

The leopard is a solitary beast
And smaller than other big cats like tigers and lions
But its slightly shorter forelegs have immense leaping strength
It has been fashioned to climb trees and its eyes can see in the dark

For three months the cub was fed at the breast
No beast nor snake ever attacked
No male leopard feasted on it — and finally
The cub was turning adult

The time was coming for mother and daughter to part

And when her offspring started to attract males with her scent
The mother leopard did not hide her hostility
So even before she was taught how to hunt
The daughter was banished, separated even from her brothers

To fill her empty belly, she hunted each day, only to escape back up trees
Then the moment she pinned down her first prey
And tore the soft throat of that stray fawn
Her mouth was dyed in the rouge of blood

She was twelve when her mother died
And not yet mature in either mind or body
And though it is unfortunate to lose a mother
It may not amount to unhappiness
That as adult females
They did not end up hating each other

母と娘

嵯峨京子

群れをつくらない豹は
同じネコ科の虎やライオンに比べ
中型でやや短い前脚と優れた跳躍力で
木登りに適した身体と夜でも見える眼を与えられた

3ヶ月ものあいだ乳を与え
獣や蛇に襲われることもなく
牡の豹にも喰われず　ようやく
大人になりかけた子供だった

豹の母娘に別れの時がやってくる

娘の豹が牡を惹きつける匂いを放ち始めると
母親の豹はあからさまに敵意をみせた
まだ狩りの仕方も教わらないうちに
娘の豹は兄弟とも別れ群れから追放された

空腹を満たすために何度も狩りに挑んでは樹上に逃げ帰る日々
初めて狩りに成功した瞬間
群れからはぐれた小鹿の柔らかい喉元を喰いちぎった赤い血が
娘の豹の口元を紅のように染めた

娘は　12歳で母と死別した
心も体も未熟なままで
母親を亡くすことは不運ではあるけれど
大人になって女同士
疎まれることもなかったのは
不幸とは言えないだろう

SAITOH Akinori

The Mind's Eyes And Ears

2020 saw the 250th anniversary of Beethoven's birth
Even after losing his sense of hearing
He scored down the sounds his mind's ears caught
And the harmony of voice and sound became his *Ninth Symphony*

Monet suffered from cataract in old age
And could see almost nothing
Yet with the light in his mind as his oils
The harmony of light and colour became his 'Water Lilies'

And Tchaikovsky's *Swan Lake*
Saved Miyamoto Amon from withdrawing from the world
And trying to picture music
Miyamoto became a stage producer

In my childhood I had tympanitis in the right ear
And lost almost all my hearing in it
Though an operation for cataract last year
Has made the world brighter now

And as I pen these poems I wonder
If I am capturing the world of language
As sharply as the inner ear of Beethoven
Or as clearly as the inner eye of Monet

It is not music, nor light, nor hands
That weave words into verse — but thought or reason perhaps
Or perhaps, as Pascal believed, a world divorced of reason
Or the delusion of *klistamano*; or *alaya* — the core of all consciousness

心の眼・心の耳

斉藤明典

2020 年はベートーベンの生誕 250 周年だった
彼は　耳が聞こえなくなっても
心の耳に聞こえる音を楽譜に書いて
声と音の調和「第九」を創り出した

モネは晩年　白内障を患って
ほとんど眼が見えなくなったが
心の中の光を絵の具にして
光と色の調和　「睡蓮」を描いた

チャイコフスキーの「白鳥の湖」は
ひきこもり状態の宮本亜門を救い出した
彼は　音楽を視覚化しようと
演出家になった

ぼくは子どもの頃　右耳が中耳炎にかかり
片方は聴力がほとんどなくなった
眼の方は昨年　白内障の手術を受けて
以前より世界が明るくなった

ぼくは　詩を書いている　が
ベートーベンの　心の耳
モネの　心の眼ほどに感じ取り
言葉の世界を高めることができているだろうか

言葉…文字を紡ぐのは手ではない
音でもない　光でもない　想いと理性？
パスカルの言った　理性の知らない領域？
それとも　第 7 末那識？　第 8 阿頼耶識？

None of Us

None of us
In this world
Stands on an easy spot
Each is a clumsy acrobat
Walking his or her tightrope

None of us
In this world
Has gone without any loss
Often something precious
Is taken away from us

Then
Is it wrong if I tell you
I love you?
I am talking to you, my friend
Friend by my side
Even if we have not met
Even if we never meet
A soulmate living somewhere in this world
Walking a tightrope and clinging onto life
I'm talking to you as a soulmate

誰ひとりとして

わたしたちはこの世で
誰ひとりとして
たやすいところに立ってはいない
細い綱の上を渡る
じつに不器用な軽業師である

わたしたちはこの世で
誰ひとりとして
何も失わなかったひとはいない
大切な何かは
しばしばどこかへ運びさられた

だから
あなたを愛すると
言ってはいけないだろうか
友よ　あなたのことだ
かたわらにいる友
たとえまだ会ったことがなくても
永遠に会うことはなくても
どこかで生きている友
命がけで細い綱の上を渡っている
私とよく似たあなたのことだ

Reminiscence — Today It Starts —

SASAKI Yutaka

I went to a festival of children's poems in Nagoya,
And one event was for the recitation of original work.
I also listened to 'Today it starts' by Tomoko Takamaru,
A familiar piece from primary school textbooks,
It had been put to music by a teacher and sung by the poet and
   friends.
As we listened, my friend, her shoulders trembling, began to cry.
   A sound that no one knows,
   That shatters this shell of mine,
   Something starts today,
   Something that is good.
It encourages those who suffered the events of 3.11
   and the victims of Niigata Chuetsu Earthquake;
And now it plants itself in the heart of a friend
   who just wants to run away from her troubles —
   So happy we have met,
   And in the heart,
   A sudden thrill,
   I notice I am here —
   A sound that no one knows,
   That shatters this shell of mine,
   Something starts today,
   Something that is good.
And, hoping it will bring strength, I listen and pray.

思い出 — 今日からはじまる —

佐々木　豊

名古屋の子どもの詩のフェスティバルに出かけた。

自作の詩を朗読するプログラムがあった。

高丸さんの「今日からはじまる」を聴いた。

小学校の教科書にも載っている馴染みのある作品だ。

小学校の音楽教師が曲をつけた歌として、高丸さんたちがお披露目された。

「今日からはじまる」の歌を聴いているうちに、友人は肩を震わせて、涙を落とし始めた。

　　　—だれも知らない音だけど

　　　　わたしの殻をやぶる音

　　　　今日からはじまる

　　　　何かいいこと—

3・11で被害に遭われた方々を、また、新潟中越沖地震で被害に遭われた方々をもこの詩は激励している。

そして、今、逃げ出したいと思っている友の心にも留まって、

　　　—わたしに会えてよかった

　　　　胸の鼓動も

　　　　ときめきも

　　　　私がいて気づいた

　　　　だれも知らない音だけど

　　　　わたしの殻をやぶる音

　　　　今日からはじまる

　　　　何かいいこと—

と、激励することなればと、祈りながら聴いていた。

The Unkempt Garden

Perhaps,
In the public's view, or by urban standards,
It's slightly off the mark — well, of course;
And in any case, it doesn't matter;
There are limits to what humans can do.

I look at the flowers,
I look at the trees —
They all lack good manners;
Even more since spring has come.
No attempt to line up or gather together;
Yet they surround the land in every nook and cranny;
They stretch out all over the ground and measure the sky,
And with remarkable speed, raise all their leaves,
    open their buds and call their adjoining flowers.
They greet us from a distant world, for this land is human owned,
"But be sure to show due respect, everyone."
They offer fragrant presents to forgetful passers-by.
Announcing, "This is a garden."
— Yes, a careless 'court' —
"But feel free to look."

"How nice to meet you!"
The worn greetings of men flit about,
Some in a hurry and angry about being forced to make a detour,
"What an unkempt garden —
And it talks to us without being asked!"
"Oh, I know. It's a problem, indeed."
At that time, let us respond,
"What problem? This amount of lack of care is just fine."
For your sake — as human beings.

気ままな庭

いささか
世間感覚から都市認識から
ずれているが当たり前にある
どうってことはない
人間が手を着けた境界はある

花を見る
樹木を見る
どれも行儀良くない
春が来たのでなおさらだ
整列や集合を試みた気配もない
しかしその土地を隅々まで囲っている
彼らはいっせいに地表に伸び上がり空を測る
めきめきと葉を立ち上げ　蕾を開き隣花を呼ぶ
人間から遠い世界があいさつをする　人間の所有地で
（人間はあらゆる配慮をしてください）
忘れっぽい通行人には香りを贈る
「ここは庭です」
どうってことはない　「庭」です
（けれど視線をどうぞ）

（あ　はじめまして）
人間の疲れたあいさつは飛びはねる
急ぎ足の誰かが回り道をさせられたことに憤る
「なんて　気ままな庭なんだ
わたしたちに　自分から話しかけてくるよ」
「まったく　実に　問題だ」
その時　答えよう
「何が？　いいですよ　このくらいの気ままは」
人であるあなた自身のために

Going To See You

When sad
I go
To see you
Biting your lip
Under the cherry tree

When glad
I go
To see you
The first time you entered the sea
And danced with distant waves

When lonely
I go
To see you
Watching the red sunset turn purple
Looking at the street corner for your mother

When lost
I go
To see you
Waiting with anxious hands
To sound just once the final cymbals

I go
To see you
As if we were living the same hours
To meet that same me
That was once a child

会いにゆく

かなしいとき
わたしは会いにゆく
桜の木の下で
くちびるをかみしめている
あなたに

うれしいとき
わたしは会いにゆく
はじめて海に入って
遠くから来た波と踊っている
あなたに

さみしいとき
わたしは会いにゆく
赤から紫に変わる夕焼けを見て
曲り角に母の姿を探している
あなたに

迷っているとき
わたしは会いにゆく
合奏の最後に一度だけ鳴らすシンバルを
汗の手で握って待っている
あなたに

わたしは会いにゆく
まるで同じ時間を生きているように
会いにゆく
子どものころの
わたしに

Anonymous Monument

Let us build a monument
In memory of the thousand and more who have died
And for all the bereaved families who want to pray for them
Let us raise a memorial
No need to engrave their names
For, sadly, many do not want it to be known —
They died of COVID-19
The nurse who placed the corpse in its sack
Regrets
She could not even wipe the body
Her feelings of regret and our consolation and gratitude
The body went straight to the crematorium
And, to avoid domestic infections and close contact, with no
    family attending,
They just embrace the urn of bones returned to them
Only one in ten can be hospitalized
Bereaved families say they are thankful
Just for this
Can you believe it?
Such a huge thing
Is not the right to hospitalization basic?
Is not the right to treatment basic?
This is Japan!
Though it seems not —
Not when Osaka suffered its fourth wave
So for the many who died
And to admonish our failed administration
Let us build this anonymous memorial
That their lives will never be forgotten
Let us raise a memorial to all their dead souls

無記名の慰霊碑

島　秀生

慰霊碑を建てよう
千人を超える人が亡くなった
祈りたい遺族はたくさんいるから
慰霊碑を建てよう
死没者の
名前は記さなくてよい
残念ながら
親族がコロナで亡くなったことを
知られたくない人は多い
納体袋に入れてくれたのは看護師さん
体を拭いてあげることもできなかったと
悔いてくれるけど
その気持ちが嬉しいよ　ありがとう
火葬場に直行だった
家庭内感染や濃厚接触者の家族は立ち会うことも叶わずに
帰ってきた骨を抱きしめるばかり
十人に一人しか入院できない中
うちは入院できただけ幸せですと
遺族が言う
そんな莫迦なこと
入院できるのは当たり前だろう
治療してもらえるのは当たり前だろう
ここは日本だぞ！
当たり前を
されることがなかった大阪の新型コロナ第四波
亡くなったたくさんの人のために
失敗を犯した行政を戒めるために
無記名の慰霊碑を建てよう
忘れてはいけない多くの人生のために
慰霊碑を建てよう

SHIMOMAE Koichi

A Crepuscular Morning

April,
The autistic metropolis,

In the deserted street,
The belch of low, bass-pitched horns,

Aggravating anxiety.

Blocked up within the well,
A time for self-restraint,

We rotate on our axes,

Some unfathomable entity
Charging us with its requests.

Down the world's history of lockdown,
The spirit of social decency
Dislodged like an avalanche.

No clusters, no close contact, no rooms unventilated

A call to avoid our three dense states,
Calling into the void to each other;

In the dim light of morning,

We have been infected —
Already and deeply.

薄明かりの朝

四月
自閉する都市

人気のない街路に
超低音の警笛が鳴り渡る

すさぶ不安

井の中の閉塞に
自粛する時

私たちは自転する

計り知れないものに
ただ要請されて

ロックダウンの世界史に
世間体の精神が
なだれ落ちていく

「密集・密接・密閉」

三密の出立を
人知れず虚に呼び交わす

薄明かりの朝

私たちはすでに
そして深く感染している

Call Me Amanda

Here I am looking through the glass at people passing by
My sisters no longer by my side
And unknown faces all around

Mother's advice came to mind
"You need to show your beauty at its peak
If you want to marry well and early"

A young woman came in and sighed, "What a beautiful shade of pink!"
Her shining eyes pressing closer to the roses beside me
"Her name is Bellavita," explained the saleswoman with a smile
The glass door was opened and she was picked out for marriage

Then the door was closed tightly shut again
Life is comfortable here and as I dozed off
The greenhouse in the mountains where I grew up appeared
And my parents and sisters and all my friends
With whom I had spent calm, happy days

Then suddenly I was woken to the store thronging with busy people
And I wondered how long had passed

Someone was staring at me from outside
"I am Amanda!" I cried as loud as I could through the glass
"Don't you find me beautiful? Any day now my bright red, sweet-
    smelling flowers will open!
Please take me home with you. For my name stands for *I love you*!"

Both arms laden with shopping bags
The lady looked at me for a time
Then went her way without coming any closer

わたしの名前はアマンダ

白井ひかる

気がつくとガラス越しに行き交う人々の姿が見える
一緒にいたはずの姉や妹の姿が見当たらない
周りを見渡すと知らない顔ぶればかりだ

『早く良いところにお嫁に行くには
せいぜい自分を美しく見せることが大切なのよ』
私は母の言葉を思い出していた

「きれいなピンク色ね」　店に入ってきた若い女性が
瞳を輝かせながら私の隣の薔薇に顔を近づけた
「ベラヴィータといいます」　店員が微笑みながら答えた
硝子戸は開けられ　彼女は抜き取られ　お嫁に行ってしまった

再び硝子戸はぴったり閉ざされた
ここはとても居心地が良い　うつらうつらしていると
生まれ育った山間のビニールハウスでの生活が甦る
両親や姉妹や大勢の仲間たち
いつも一緒に過ごした穏やかな日々…

店内のざわつく音で私ははっと目を覚ました
百貨店は慌ただしく混雑している　どれほど時間が経ったのだろう

その時私は通路からじっとこちらを見つめる視線に気が付いた
『わたしの名前はアマンダ！』　硝子戸越しに私は力の限り叫んだ
『綺麗でしょう？　もうすぐ真っ赤に花開くのよ　甘い香りもするわ
どうぞお家に連れて行って　花言葉は "あなたを愛している" なの』

両手に重そうな買い物袋を提げたその女の人は
しばらくの間わたしを見つめてくれたけど
近づくことなくどこかへ行ってしまった

"Others Are Others..."

That means that,
This means this.

On the outskirts of town,
Dusk on a chilly autumn evening.

> *tsuzure sase*
> *sase sase tsuzure*

I amble amidst this brocade of insect song,
Hearing but not listening.

The knack of distancing oneself,
I was told, is not to care about what others think.

"Others are others; and I am myself,
Above all, go the way of the self." *

The enlightened by words of a philosopher
Carved in stone.

And unawares, it has become
My motto — and my spell.

* This poem appears on a stone monument in Kyoto to the philosopher
NISHIDA Kitaro, who wrote *A Study of Good, The Path of Philosophy*.

「人は人…」

白川　淑

それはそれ
これはこれ

町はずれの
秋さむの　夕ぐれ

つづれ　させ
させ　させ　つづれ

集く虫の声　つれて
きくともなしの　そぞろあるき

人ばなれの　こつは
わりきること　と教えられ

「人は人　吾はわれ也
　とにかくに　吾行く道を　吾は行くなり」

碑の
哲人の言葉に　諭され

いつの間にやら
呪文みたいに　口癖に

＊歌碑 ― 哲学者　西田幾多郎『善の研究』
　　　　洛東　哲学の道

99

Nandina Leaves

In the late autumn
The nandina leaves
Had not yet turned red
And still no change in December
I worried if they would turn
Within a month

But New Year was celebrated
With the nandina still green
And even at *setsubun**
Not a hint of red

March came
With warm spring sunlight
And autumn deepened
With the leaves still stubbornly green
Then winter
And spring
But they never turned
Though new sprouts grew

Looking up at the sky
Or at our clothes
Or supermarket shelves
Or people in the street
No signs of seasonal change
Plants cannot see the future
But I worry what will become of us

* A festival in February that marks the end of winter.

ナンテン

園田恵美子

晩秋のころ
ナンテンの葉の色が
かわらないのに気がついた
12月になっても
まだかわらない
1ヶ月以内で赤くなるか心配だった

お正月に緑のナンテンで
新年をむかえた
節分になっても
気配すら感じられない

3月になって
春の日ざしを感じるころも
晩秋のナンテンのままである
冬が来て
春が来て
赤くならないナンテン
それでも新芽が出た

空を見ても
服を見ても
スーパーマーケットにも
道行く人にも
季節を感じられない
先が見えない植物達
これから何が起こるのか

Excerpts from *Ayara Kinshū* — Mixed Twill Cloth

Village of Niutsuhime
Like a rippling river under a blue sky and dancing cotton clouds
Hosts of heavenly red spider lilies stretch to the mountain fields
of golden-harvested rice

The Season Lingers
Under a pale blue sky crossed by migratory birds, with no sight
and no hearing,
Rabbit Dog* at the close of her life searching for a buzzing cicada

Fading —
Under the light blue sky and rays of red from sunset clouds
The hoarse voice of a late cicada seeps from a great cherry tree
Its yellow leaves fluttering down remnants of the fading summer

A Noble Woman's Dream
In a room filled with the aroma of fragrant olives
An Autumn Goddess tickles the nose of my sleeping Rabbit Dog
How dearly she wakes, her gaze wandering the heavens...

Supper of The Gods
The sepia scenery of persimmons hanging at the modern hospital
windows
Emerge from the late autumn light to touch this battered heart
and make it tremble

First-Year *Bon*** Festival
An album the weight of nineteen years of a thousand gold pieces
Both Rabbit Dog with her carefree smile and I will fade away in time
Day by day, fading away, you are beautiful
The eyes of your withering body divine and full of compassion
The years cannot steal the light lodged in your heart

* Rabbit Dog: my beloved rabbit-like toy poodle, Vone
* * *Bon* is an annual festival when the spirits of the dead are said to return to earth

綾羅錦 綉 <ruby>綾<rt>あや</rt></ruby><ruby>羅<rt>ら</rt></ruby><ruby>錦<rt>きんしゅう</rt></ruby>　　　　（一部抜粋）

丹生都比売の里 <ruby>丹<rt>に</rt></ruby><ruby>生<rt>う</rt></ruby><ruby>都<rt>つ</rt></ruby><ruby>比<rt>ひめ</rt></ruby><ruby>売<rt></rt></ruby>の<ruby>里<rt>さと</rt></ruby>
綿雲が踊る青空の下でさざめく川のように
黄金色の稲穂が刈られた田圃から累々と山へ続く曼珠沙華は天上の花

なずむ季節
渡り鳥が行き交う水色の空の下で視力も聴力もないのに
鳴いてるツクツク法師を探すうさぎ犬の終わりつつ命…

うつろひ…
水色の空に茜さす雲の下で
桜の大木から老いたツクツク法師嗄れ鳴けば
黄葉舞い散るハラハラ消えゆく夏の残滓

貴婦人の夢
金木犀の香り満たされた部屋で
秋の女神が眠り深きうさぎ犬の鼻をこそばゆぅ
目覚めて宙を彷徨う姿が愛し…

神々の饗餐
近代的な病院の窓の下で柿がたわわになっているセピア色の風景が
晩秋の光で浮かび上がり荒む心が感動に震える

初盆
19年いう歳月に千金の重み気づかされたアルバムの中で
屈託なく笑ううさぎ犬と　あたいもいつしか色褪せてく
日々色褪せていく君は美し
枯れ果てていく身から慈愛に満ちた眼差しは神々しい
歳月は心の輝きまで奪えず

　　　うさぎ犬（Rabbit Dog）＝兎によく似たTプードルの愛犬『ヴォーン』

A Red Blaze of Canna Flowers

TAJIMA Hiroko

One autumn, when I was in my final year at high school,
  and mother wept at having three of us to send to college,
I entered the nursing school attached to Osaka National Hospital where
  I only had to pay for books.
    "Tak' a taxi frae the station. Yer a country lass,"
She told me, laughing at her broad dialect;
Then pushed some bank notes into my bellyband with her chapped hands.
I bought my ticket by working one of the two weeks of summer holiday.
Nineteen hours on a steam train, closing the windows at tunnels,
My nostrils and hair black with soot;
    And then, on the main Miyazaki Line,
A red blaze of canna flowers came into view,
And I vowed that one day I would bloom like them.

Then working part-time at an eye clinic — with its smell of cresol —
I sent my parents my first salary as a nurse —
Always exposed to the sun, a farmer's back suffers heat rashes,
His humble table is devoid of luxury, and there are no new clothes —
This made me into a woman who does not like defeat,
And at thirty I was made Head Nurse to a National Hospital.
My eldest son was six, his brother four,
    So I started after-school care for latchkey kids.
Four years later, I had my first daughter,
    Heard her crying, and heard her laughter.
    "The Head Nurse having a baby! Never heard such nonsense!"
The surgical manager shouted furiously.
Head Nurses were all single. But one who was married told me,
    "Don't give up your post. Keep on working.
      Take breaks to breast-feed your baby,
      And tell the same to all your nurses."
She was like a mother to me.
I was the first to take these breaks, going home an hour early,
So I breastfed my daughter — the age of married heads had arrived —
The tears built up and spilled over,
My red blaze of canna flowers had finally bloomed.

真っ赤に燃えるカンナの花

田島廣子

高校三年の秋三人大学に出すのは苦しがね母は泣いた
国立大阪病院附属の看護学校に入学本代だけ全て無料
　　大阪駅に着いたらタクシーでいっとよ　田舎もん
母は金を腹巻きに入れ強く巻いた　あかぎれに触れた
ふるさとの言葉丸出しで喋って　笑っていた
夏休みは二週間一週間はアルバイト切符を買った
石炭で走る汽車に十九時間トンネルで窓を閉め
髪も鼻の穴もすす　宮崎の線路沿いに
真っ赤に燃えて咲くカンナをみていた
私も　いつかカンナの花のように咲きたい

眼科医院でアルバイト　クレゾールの匂い
看護婦になり初めての給料は　両親に送った
百姓さんの背中はいつも太陽の下　あせもだ
美味しいもの　新しい服はなく質素な暮らし
その姿が　私を負けず嫌いに育てていった
三十歳　国立療養所近畿中央病院婦長に昇任
長男六歳次男四歳鍵っ子学童保育所を作った
三十四歳長女誕生赤子の声と笑い声がした
　　婦長がどこに妊娠する奴がおるか
外科部長は　怒り狂って言った
独身の婦長ばかり　所帯持ちの婦長が言った
　　看護婦を辞めたらいかん　続けて働くんよ
　　婦長さん授乳時間を取って下さい
　　あなた達もとりなさいと言ってほしい
と　看護部長は言った　母のように思えた
私が一番に授乳時間をとり一時間早く帰り
母乳で育てた　所帯持ち婦長の時代が来た
私は涙が込み上げてきて泣いた
真っ赤に燃えてカンナの花が咲いていた

On A Sunny Day

I spread my arms
And take a deep breath

As if summoning
Distant friends
I call and
The azure sky fills
My outstretched heart

And if sometimes lost
And sometimes the heart feels cramped
Surely it is so that I can bound
Into the blue sky of today

On such a day
A voice is calling me to leap
Higher and higher
With the soul of a newborn child
And I feel I can go anywhere
Free as the spirit takes me

Set to music by the composer Takahiro Abe (Kawai Publishing)

晴れた日に

高丸もと子

両手を広げて
深呼吸をする

オーイと
遠くにいる友だちを
呼ぶかっこうだ
伸ばした心に
青空もいっしょに入ってくる

迷ったり
心を縮めたりしていたのは
きっと
今日のような青空へ
バウンドするためのもの

もっともっと
はねてみないか
こんな日
うまれたての気分になって
自由にどこへでも
行けそうな気がする

作曲：アベタカヒロ（カワイ出版）

Bullet Train Needlework

The Bullet Train flows along
Through fabric-like scenery
Sewing rain scene to fair
And mountain scene to open field

On and on, piece by piece
At super express speed
And when it arrives at its terminus
What will the patchwork look like?

Its flowing movement
Faster than any other machine

It enters a tunnel
Where black cloth awaits

And when it emerges
There is a different coloured thread
Of fog flowing down the mountain

The fabric that started at the first station
Is checked at major stops like Kyoto and Nagoya
And when it arrives in Tokyo
What will the finished cloth look like?
Or is its patchwork still in progress?

新幹線の針仕事

武西良和

新幹線が流れるように走る
さまざまな情景はまるで布模様だ
雨を縫い晴れを縫う
そして山地を縫い平地を縫う

さまざまな布を時速250キロの
スピードで縫い続けていくと
終着駅に着いたころ
どんな布に仕上がるのか

新幹線の動きは
どんな機械よりも速いに違いない

まもなく電車がトンネルに入る
黒い布がそこで待っている

トンネルを出ると
霧が山から下りて来た
新しい縫い糸が用意されている

始発駅から縫い始められた布は
京都や名古屋などの主な駅で点検される
東京駅に着いたとき
どんな布に仕上がっているのだろう
それともまだ仕事途中なのか

Listening to Glen Gould

TANAKA Shinji

Glenn Gould's Mozart,
On side A of my disk —
A piece entitled
'Piano Sonata No.11, in A major
With Turkish March' —
An eighteen-minute performance
That gives a faint sense of loneliness
Without articulating it.

グレン　グールドを聴く

田中信爾

グレン　グールドのモーツァルト
そのＡ面
「ピアノソナタ第11番　イ長調」
「トルコ行進曲つき」
という名のある曲
約18分の演奏である
それはそこはかとなく孤独を感じさせる
孤独を言うことも出来ずに ── 。

TONOMURA Bunsho

Greeting The New Year

New Year spent amidst coronavirus,
At a *soba* noodle restaurant at Kusatsu Station,
After a meeting of our painting group,
Because the annual party has been cancelled,
I'm throwing one alone at the usual venue.

I order a glass of local Kinkame *sake*,
And deep-fried oysters,
And toast to another spirited year and for a little peace of mind,
As the lively young girls serve their customers.

Will the Tokyo Olympic Games
Be held this summer without incident?
And in the autumn,
Will the family of our second daughter
Return from California
With our granddaughter who has just started school?

It all seems to depend
On the arrival of the vaccine;
So I go on in hope,
Towards my special 88th *beiju* birthday,
With a collection of essays to be published in May.

86 years of life —
With no regrets;
Years passed in satisfaction,
As I face my term.

新しい年を迎える

コロナ禍の中の新年
近江の草津駅前のそば屋で
絵の勉強会が終了して
今年は新年会が中止となった
いつもの店で　ひとり新年会

地元の酒　金亀と
かきフライを注文して
今年も元気にと　ひとときの安らぎ
溌剌とした女性店員の姿

夏の東京オリンピックは
無事に開催できるのか
秋にはアメリカ　カルフォルニアから
二女の家族が
小学校一年生の孫娘が
帰国できるだろうか

すべてはワクチンの
到着次第のようで
希望を持って進みたい
米寿をめざして
５月にはエッセイ集が上梓される

86年の人生を生きて
悔いることがなかったと
満足して過ごせた年月
いま終末を迎えている

A Broken Twig of Blossom

A broken-off twig of cherry
I placed in a glass and admired a while
Then one petal fell floating down
Onto the surface of the water

The red-yellow of the pollen on its stamens
The swollen ovary engraved behind its center
And the light red flower lips the shape of a heart
A five-petaled flower with no trace of imperfection
Its delicate pattern so lovely in contrast
To the majestic appearance of the tree

Just before I had plucked the irresistible twig from its branch
Tempted first by the exquisite blossoms seen from the third floor
    of a large bookstore
Then more from the glass window of a detour to Takashimaya
And still more from the overhead walkway I passed over
At Sakaidani Nakadori on my way home

Yet floating in its glass
The purity of its petals
Blames no one
Hates no one
Accepting whatever passing time may bring

It just reflects —
Not long ago
I was part of that majestic scene
A single blossom adding praise to the grace of spring
And even if no one had broken me off
The time to flutter and fall comes inevitably

花折れ

司 由衣

折れた桜の小枝を
ガラスコップに挿してしばらく見入っている
と　花びら一輪はらりと落ちて
水面に浮かんだ

雄蕊の薬粉の紅黄色
花心の奥の膨れた子房
薄紅さす花唇はハートの形に似て
寸分の乱れもない五弁の花びら
そのこまやかな花模様は
桜木の雄々しい姿から窺い知れない可憐さで

つい先ほど　大型書店の三階から
そのあと寄り道した高島屋のガラス窓から
そして通り抜けてきた歩道橋からも眺めた
境谷中通りの桜並木
その爛漫の花に見惚れて思わず手折った一枝

それでも
ガラスコップに浮かんだ
花の潔さは
誰も咎めず　厭わず
時の経過を　その仕打ちを受け入れている

ふと　思いが過ぎる
かつてわたしも
いま目にした雄々しい桜木の
奢りの春を謳歌している花の一輪だったのだと
誰かに手折られなくても
はらはらと落下のときは必ず来ることを ──

Corona And This Abnormal Life

USHIRO Keiko

I wear a mask every day when I go out
Sweaty and stuffy in the midsummer heat
I push it under my chin in a residential area where no one is out
They say to remove the mask from one ear to drink water
But dangling it from one ear makes me uneasy
It might fly off as if blown away by the wind.

Even if they tell us to handle the mask carefully
Because it may have the virus on it
As I get older and with my bags, my movements become sluggish
And I just cannot do everything as instructed
Going home and washing my hands carefully
Hanging my jacket in the hall
Washing glasses I have not washed
And then taking a bath? I just cannot do it
My body cannot cope with all this absurdity.

If I could see the virus, I could kill it with antiseptic
I'm sure I'm desperately wiping things completely free of it
And I always disinfect my hands at the entrance of any store
But my hands get rough because I repeat this a dozen times a day
I think I'd been unlucky if I got it so I am not behaving paranoically
But I'm elderly and I have to be prepared for death
So I avoid going out into crowds.

There are no teas after our meetings
And when asked to wear a mask so friends can chat after a meal
I lose the will to speak because my hearing is bad
With so many restrictions it becomes difficult just to live
And I find myself asking how long this virus-dictated life will last.

コロナ禍の異常な生活

後　恵子

外出するときは毎日マスクをつけ
真夏の暑さに汗だくで息苦しい
人が歩いていない住宅街では顎の下に押しやる
片耳からマスクを垂らしたままは不安
風に吹かれるように飛んでいく

ウイルスがついているかもしれないから
マスクの扱いを慎重にと説かれても
荷物を持って歳とって動作が鈍くなって
指示通りにはとてもできない
家に帰って手を入念に洗って
上着を玄関のところに置いて
洗ったことのない眼鏡を洗って
入浴してなどできない
私には突飛な行動で身体は壊れる

ウイルスが見えるなら消毒液で殺せるのに
ウイルスのいないところを必死に拭いているだろう
店の入り口で必ず手を消毒している
一日何十回も消毒液を使うから手は荒れる
罹患したら運が悪いのだと神経質な行動をしていないが
高齢者なので死を覚悟しなければならないから
人込みの中に行くのは避けている

会合のあとのお茶の時間はどこもなくなった
友人との食事後のお喋りもマスクをつけるように言われると
耳の悪くなった私は喋る気力を失う
制限が多くなって生きるのが苦しくなって
ウイルスに振り回される生活がいつまで続くのだろうか

Signs

Someone calls me
And stopping in my tracks
Drops of rain rolling down
Hydrangea leaves
Reflecting sorrow
Lifted from me

Someone touches me
And turning round
See the flower
Swaying in the breeze
Nodding clearly to me
Sending me onward
As if it were you

気配

山本由美子

呼びかけられて
立ち止まると
紫陽花の葉に
雫が転がる
引き受けた
悲しみを映して

触れられて
振り向くと
吹き抜ける風に
いつかの花が揺れている
大きく頷いて
送り出してくれた
あなたのように

The Chestnut Grove

The hundred-and-ten-year-old chestnuts confront me;
"All that is left now are our trunks and their withered and
    weakened branches.
No strength to bear leaves or fruit. What would you do with us?
You can cut us down from the base if that is your wish."

"But I cannot do that! Born in the first year of Meiji,
This grove was the lifework of our grandfather.
Just as always, watch over our household as part of the family —
You are the treasuries of our memories, how are we to cut you
    from your roots?"

Since childhood, each autumn we enjoyed chestnut gathering —
The grove across from the house, the chirp of birdsong, and great
    buckets of large, glossy nuts that we delivered to the main
    kitchen —
During post-war days when chocolate had not yet appeared in
    most towns.

Back then, the grove would make suggestions to us:
"Come up into our branches… Make a swing to play on…"
So I climbed halfway up a tree with strong, easily manageable branches,
And, all by myself, hung a strong rope to make a swing on a
    sturdy branch stretching straight out from the trunk.

Around my feet, grew wild mums and violet gentians,
    And yuzuri leaves that all looked quietly up at the sky.
I got on the suspended rope and, swinging back and forth,
A voice whispered, "How refreshing to think up stories surrounded
    by nature."
And to this day that voice remains, as the old trees age year by year.

After more than seventy years, the indubitable voice still lives in
    my spine and in this hand that writes.

栗林

安森ソノ子

樹齢百十年の栗の樹木は　私に問う
「幹と　枯れて弱くなった枝を残すのみとなりました
葉も実もつける活力が無い　　どうなさいますか老木たちを
根本から切る決心をして下さっても良いのですよ」と

「いや　この栗林は　明治元年に生まれた祖父の作品そのものです
伐採するなんて　　できません
今迄どおりわが家を見守って　家族同様の心で居てほしい
思い出詰まる宝庫の主である其方たち　根本から切るなんて駄目」

子供の頃より　秋の栗拾いを楽しんだ
自宅の向かいの栗林　野鳥のさえずり身に近く　つややかに光る大き
　な栗の実を　たくさん集めて母屋の台所に置いた
チョコレートなど多くの街に出まわっていない敗戦後の月日

その頃　自家の栗林は言い出した　「木に登らないか　それともブラ
　ンコを作って遊んでは？」と
登りやすい枝ぶりの栗の木へは　途中まで登って行った
横に長く張り出した太い枝に丈夫な縄をかけ　一人で作った手製のブ
　ランコ

足もとに自生の野菊　紫色の竜胆　ゆずり葉たちがしずかに空を仰ぐ
栗の木に吊るした縄のみを使ったブランコに乗り　揺れている時
「こんな自然の中で物語の筋を考えたら　爽快だろうな」との声湧い
　てきた　　同じ声は今日まで消えず　栗の古木は老いるばかり

七十年以上経った今　その確かな招き　ものを書かしめ脊柱に宿る

Catch Ball

Released from one man's hand, the ball
Lifts in an arc against the sunset sky over the fountain square

Two men who had been talking together just now
Beside this bench, baseball gloves in hand

Perhaps they are childhood friends
Playing catch ball and exchanging lonely remarks

"How long do you think we have left?"
"All I ask is that you don't go before me."

"But you have no worries. My wife went before me.
You can't imagine how empty life is without her!"

And like the two men's futures
The ball arches in their anxious lines of vision

The ball received in one glove is thrown back to the other
Drawing bonding arcs between their two lives —

And until it reaches the friend's glove
Oh, the long, dazzling moment of its condensed journey.

キャッチボール

吉田定一

男の手から離れたボールが
噴水広場の夕焼け空に　弧を描いてとびかう

座っているベンチの傍で　先ほどグローブを手にして
ことばを交わしていた男たちだ

お互い幼馴染であるらしく
淋しいことばのキャッチボールをしていた

「もう何年　生きておられるだろうか」
「おい！　俺より先に逝くなよ」

「だけどお前はいいさ　おれは女房に先立たれての
なんと淋しい暮らしをしていることか」

二人の男たちの　これからの生のように
行くさき不安な視線の中をボールがとびかう

グローブで受け止めたボールが投げ返される
二人の人生の絆のように　弧を描いて……

ボールが　相手のグローブに届くまでの
ああ　なんと長いまばゆい　一瞬の旅路だことか ──

Schools And Their Pupils in COVID
—— How Undefeated They Live!

All schools required by the government to close as of March 2, 2021.

March — the climax the school year. The time when all is concluded. The sixth graders the worst hit. The culmination of six years of elementary school life. Preparations for the graduation ceremony just about to start. And then their school required to shut down. No assurance of a ceremony. No time to say their farewells to friends or teachers. And then, two weeks later, the sudden promise that graduation alone would go ahead.

Normally, they would practice hard for the ceremony, but this year there could be none. And, after the diplomas had been awarded, they lined up in tiers on the stage for a group recitation. Six years of memories, gratitude and hope. The scenarios put together by their class teachers before shutdown. Each held a copy, but no one needed it, as they recited in one great chorus before they sang the school song in full voice. Then, parading through our floral arch, they all graduated. And from the proud party of parents and teachers, full of admiration came the refrain, "Children are just amazing!"

In April, each moved a grade up, with a new class and a new class teacher. But they could hardly see each other. Then, in June, classes finally resumed. Summer holidays were cut to a fortnight to make up lost class hours. So they braved the scorching summer heat to go to school, all sweaty and wearing masks. But these children all love school. In the breaks, they run around the playground undefeated by the heat. "They all look just fine."

コロナ禍の学校と子ども達
── 子どもは、すごい

吉川悦子

　政府は３月２日から、日本全国の学校の一斉休校を要請した。

　３月は、学校にとって一番大切な時だ。１年間の締めくくりの時。特に６年生は本当にかわいそうだった。６年生にとっては小学校時代の最後の総仕上げの時である。卒業式に向けての練習もこれから始まる。そんな大事な時なのに唐突に一斉休校。卒業式もできるかどうかわからない。友達と先生と別れを惜しむ間もない。しかし二週間ほど過ぎ、卒業式だけは行われることになった。

　例年ならば、何度も練習をし当日を迎えるのだが、練習は一切無しで卒業式を迎えた。卒業証書を授与された後、６年生全員がひな壇に並び６年間の思い出や感謝、希望を込め「群読」を始めた。休校までに台本は、担任からもらっていたのだろう。みんな手に台本を持っていたのだが、誰一人台本を見ることなく堂々とした声で発表し、卒業歌も立派に歌い上げた。そして、花のアーチをくぐり、卒業していった。「子どもってすごい」　保護者も職員もただただ感動であった。

　４月、子ども達は学年が一つ上がり、新しい学級、新しい担任になったが、みんなには、なかなか会えなかった。６月からやっと授業再開。学習の遅れをとり戻すため夏休みが２週間しかなく、猛暑の中、マスクをして汗だくになりながら学校に通っている。でもみんな学校が好き。休み時間になると、暑さに負けず運動場を元気に走り回って遊んでいる。「子どもは元気だ」

Postscript

I have been given the task of writing this postscript on behalf of the team of translators.

When working as a translator of poetry, I always feel that I am committing an unknown crime without yet realizing what the exact nature of that crime actually is. What I do perceive, however, is that different languages have what we might call their own 'nature' or 'atmosphere', which cannot be satisfactorily explained simply by saying that they use different words and forms of expression. It is something that is both vague and frail, like air. Translators have to transplant this frail, airy sapling into foreign soil, a feat that is not always successful and frequently fails.

Nevertheless, the translator dares do it.

I have dared challenge this mission impossible with Professor Angus, and the other members of the team of translators, all of whom are skilled hands. I imagine they are all feeling this same kind of 'itchiness' that I do in relation to translating poetry, though we have certainly endeavoured to do justice to each poem.

Another problem is the fact that some of poems do not easily lend themselves to my approach. This may be because the poem is of too high quality. When this happens, I often feel ashamed of myself. But poets pour everything into their poetry, which means that its readers have a responsibility to do the same, and pour all of themselves into their reading of a poem.

Translation is always hard work and sometimes cruel, especially against the present background of the pandemic. We may have misunderstood the poet's intention at times. When so, please forgive our lack of experience of life. Ultimately, however, the responsibility lies on my shoulders and on my shoulders alone.

21st September, 2021
Yakushigawa Koichi

あとがき

　おわりに当たって翻訳者を代表して一言ご挨拶いたします。

　翻訳者として仕事をしていますと、否応なく、二か国語の違いを痛感いたします。それは、言葉の持っている形や表記法の違いと言うだけでなく、その言葉の周りに漂う気配と言うか、空気と言うか、風土と言うか、なんとも言えないもやもやしたものがいつまでたっても消えない感じがするのです。何とかしてそのもやもやを違う言葉に移し替えようとするのですが、うまくいった試しはありません。今回も翻訳者はどなたも靴の上から痒いところを掻いている感じが残っておられると思います。

　校正をさせて頂いている私も、アンガス先生も、完全に満足しているわけではありません。それでも何とか痒いところに指の端でも届くように努力をしてきたつもりです。

　ただ、翻訳しやすい作品と、なんともし難い作品とがあるように思います。日本語がすっきりと内容を伝えてくれない場合です。これは、読者の責任なのか、作者の責任なのか、判りません。翻訳している場合、私はいつも自分の経てきた歴史の浅薄さをひしひしと感じるのです。

　詩は、印刷された瞬間作者の手を離れて個々の読者の手にゆだねられます。作者は人手に渡った作品の責任も引き受けねばならないのですし、読者は自分の生涯のすべてを傾けて作品に向かわねばなりません。その間に立って仕事をする翻訳者の仕事は何とも罪の深いものだと、いつも痛感するのです。

　コロナが猛威を振るう中での翻訳作業は、例年と激しく異なるものでした。言い訳にはなりませんが、アンガス先生と二人でまとめの仕事をさせていただいた今年の経験は忘れがたいものとなるでしょう。

　英訳詩について様々なご批判もあろうかと思います。全ての責任は薬師川にあります。どうぞ忌憚のないご意見を賜れば幸甚に存じます。

2021 年 9 月 21 日
翻訳者一同に代わって、薬師川虹一記す

Translators:

Norman J. ANGUS:
Cambridge University, MA (Cantab.) in English Literature
Professor of Kyoto Tachibana University
Professor Emeritus, Baika Women's University

KITAOKA Takeshi:
Philosopher, Poet
Professor Emeritus of Okayama University

MIZUSAKI Noriko:
Poet, Translator, Essayist
She was Teaching English in Waseda University, Tokyo,
and others. (retired).
Member of Kansai Poets' Association, UPLI/WCP,
POV Zoom in California, etc.

SAITOH Akinori:
Poet
Member of Kansai Poets' Association

YAKUSHIGAWA Koichi:
Poet, Professor Emeritus of Doshisha University
Member of Japan Poets' Club
Member of Kyoto Photo-artists Association

YAMAMOTO Yumiko:
Poet, University Lecturer in English
Member of Japan Poets' Association
Member of Kansai Poets' Association

言葉の花火　2021

2021 年 12 月 1 日　第 1 刷発行
編集人　薬師川虹一
発行人　左子真由美
発行所　㈱ 竹林館
〒 530-0044　大阪市北区東天満 2-9-4 千代田ビル東館 7 階 FG
tel 06-4801-6111　fax 06-4801-6112
郵便振替 00980-9-44593
URL http://www.chikurinkan.co.jp
印刷・製本　モリモト印刷株式会社
〒 162-0813 東京都新宿区東五軒町 3-19

FIREWORK POEMS 2021

First published by CHIKURINKAN Dec. 2021
2-9-4-7FG, Higashitenma, Kita-ku, Osaka, Japan
http://www.chikurinkan.co.jp
Printed by MORIMOTO PRINT CO.,Ltd. Tokyo, Japan
ISBN978-4-86000-462-0　C0092